MOTIVE

A WAVERLY BEACH MYSTERY

PAMELA M. KELLEY

MOTIVE
By Pamela M. Kelley

Copyright © 2015 by Pamela M. Kelley

Please contact the author with any questions, at pamelamkelley@gmail.com

Jane Cho is a former legal investigator who returned to the seaside town of Waverly, MA to run a takeout food shop, Comfort & Joy, and to live a quiet, safer life. Jane is a cousin to David, who was in TRUST and their grandfather also has a strong supporting role, as the retired town sheriff. David's best friend, Jake, who was also a main character in TRUST, is the current sheriff.

Jane is enjoying the simpler life, but she was a really good legal investigator, before someone she was investigating tried to kill her. She thought everything was behind her as that person was convicted and is behind bars.

But one peaceful morning, Jane stumbles over a dead body while taking out the trash. The dead woman ran a nearby bed and breakfast and had been threatened by Jane's thriving new business and had even filed suit the previous week to try and shut her down.

Stranger still, someone is sending Jane cryptic messages and it's not clear if he is trying to warn her or impress her with his efforts to make her problems disappear.

1

The nightmares were back. They'd started up again about a week-and-a-half ago, out of the blue, for no apparent reason. Things were going well. Jane Cho was living her dream of running a tiny, mostly take-out food shop, cooking and baking all her favorite things. Comfort & Joy was a hit from the day the doors opened. There was nothing else like it in the small, seaside village of Waverly.

Quitting a job she loved hadn't been an easy decision, but felt like the only sensible option, given everything that had happened. Coming home to Waverly, where her grandfather was a retired sheriff and her cousin, David, lived, felt right—and safe. Jane had always loved to cook, and found the repetitive, mindless motions of chopping, dicing and stirring relaxing. It soothed her soul like nothing else.

No matter how often she reminded herself that they'd caught the killer and he would be behind bars for a very long time, it had taken a while for the nightmares to go away—but they finally did and she'd thought they were gone forever. It didn't make any sense that they were suddenly back now.

Her grandfather said it was just part of the natural transition. Now that she was settled into her new routine with the shop and things were going well, perhaps a part of her missed her former life. She had been a very good legal investigator. But, she loved running Comfort & Joy, too. Jane pushed the bothersome thoughts out of her mind and got to work, preparing for the day ahead.

For the next few hours, she made chicken pot pies, and beef stew, baked cornbread and muffins. She tossed an assortment of salads and then packaged them into individual serving boxes. She had her favorite jazzy music playing in the background and started the coffee brewing so it would be ready when the doors opened at eight a.m. for her first customers.

Her grandfather was usually one of the first to arrive, with several of his cronies. All but one were retired policemen who still kept abreast of everything going on in the small town, and discussed it at length over their morning muffins and coffee.

As she unlocked the front door and switched the closed sign to open, a cold draft blew through her hair and rattled the windowpanes. The strange sense of unease crept back again, but Jane pushed it away, determined to focus and have a good day. Melissa, her assistant, had arrived a few minutes earlier and welcomed their first customer. A moment later, her grandfather and his two buddies strolled in.

"Good morning, Janie!" he greeted her.

"Hi, Gramps." Jane smiled. Even at ninety-two, her grandfather was one of the most cheerful, positive people she knew and he always brightened her day. "The usual for you?"

Gramps glanced at his friends and they all nodded.

Jane poured their coffees and set out two corn muffins and a blueberry, all grilled with plenty of butter. Once they were set, she asked Julie to keep an eye on the front counter while she ran the trash out back to the dumpster.

She air was cold and raw as she lugged the heavy trashcan to the shed where the dumpster was. She fished in her pocket for the key, but when she looked closer saw that the shed was open and the padlock was hanging open. That was odd. It wasn't like her to forget to lock it. But, she hadn't been sleeping well all week and must have been distracted. She pushed open the door and the key dropped out of her hands.

In front of her, lying flat on the ground and looking quite dead, with a deep, bloody gash across her forehead, was Samantha Sellers. She was about Jane's age and hadn't been happy about Jane opening Comfort & Joy. She had actually just brought a lawsuit against her, trying to get the town to shut her down.

It was what Jane noticed next that sent a chill up her spine. The stiletto heel of Samantha's bright red pump had been shoved in her mouth, and stuck to the shoe was a yellow sticky note with a message written in bold, black marker,

"I took care of her for you."

2

You okay, honey? Jake should be here any minute. Maybe you should sit down?" Gramps seldom fussed over her—he wasn't the type to fuss. But he sounded worried now, and with good reason. Jane was okay, though. Just a bit shell-shocked. It was an unnerving start to her day to find a dead body sprawled by the trash.

"I'm fine, Gramps, really," Jane assured him.

"If I was in Jake's shoes and didn't know you like I do, you'd be my prime suspect. Just thought you should know that. You had motive and opportunity." Gramps had slipped into his former sheriff's persona.

Jane opened her mouth to protest, and he cut her off.

"Obviously, you had nothing to do with it. I'm just saying it looks bad. And it looks like someone wanted it to look that way. Interesting touch with the sticky note. Any thoughts on who might do something like this?"

They were standing by the dumpster and Samantha's

body. One of Gramps' buddies reached out to touch her cheek, probably curious to see what a dead person felt like and if she was really dead, but Gramps kicked his hand away. "What are you doing, Carl? You can't touch a crime scene. You could mess it all up."

Carl took a step back. "Sorry, I've just never seen anything like this before." Carl was a retired science teacher.

Jane took a deep breath and nervously waited for Jake to arrive. She hadn't seen him in many years, since high school. He was one of her cousin David's best friends and had been an award winning quarterback throughout high school. Tall, dark and classically handsome, and way out of her league. She'd admittedly had a small crush on him but he'd never noticed her.

Why would he, though? She was a freshman when he'd been a senior and, thankfully, she looked very different now than she did then. That was what she liked to think of as her awkward period.

Not that it mattered, anyway. Even if Jake was as gorgeous now as he was then, she wasn't interested. She wasn't looking for a relationship with anyone at the moment. The breakup with Nick was still too recent and too raw. For now, all her energy and focus was on making Comfort & Joy a success. And it had been going so well, until now.

"Janie Cho?" The stunning petite woman standing next to Gramps looked nothing like he remembered. The Janie he knew had been his best friend, David's, younger cousin and his last mental image of her was a scrawny, geeky girl with ugly braces, thick glasses and a ponytail. She hadn't made much of an impression.

The woman standing before him still wore a ponytail, but it was a fashionable one. The glasses and braces were gone and her mix of Korean and Caucasian features gave her an exotic wholesomeness that was very attractive.

"I'm Jane Cho. Nice to see you again, Jake."

Jake nodded to Jane, turned his attention to the elderly man at her side. "Gramps, how are you?" Jake had the greatest respect for David's grandfather. He was a legend around the station and the joke was that he was still on duty, because Gramps didn't miss a beat. He knew almost as much as Jake did about what was going on in this town, and Jake enjoyed chatting with him and bouncing ideas off him from time to time.

"Never better. Well, except for this of course. Hell of a way to start the day."

Jake got his camera out and started snapping pictures of the crime scene. Then he walked over to Janie and Gramps.

"The rest of the team should be along any minute, and they'll finish up with the body. Why don't you take me through what happened?"

"There's not much of a story. We'd just opened for the day. I was taking out the trash, and there she was. My key is missing, and the door was unlocked. That's all I know."

Jake frowned. There had to be more to the story. "That's it? Nothing else you can recall?"

Jane appeared to be thinking for a moment and then said, "No, nothing. Sorry."

"Okay. Well, let's talk about the deceased, then. Do you know her?"

"Samantha Sellers. Yes, I know her." Her tone was clipped, and Jake paused his pen and looked up. This was interesting. Jane knew Samantha and, quite clearly, did not like her.

"How do you know her?"

"She filed a lawsuit against me last week."

"Why?" He didn't like that everything he'd heard so far seemed to work to establish a motive for Jane.

"She is going through a bitter divorce, and she and her soon to be ex-husband used to run a bed and breakfast together two blocks from here. It has a small restaurant that is also open to the public for breakfast and lunch. She wanted him to sign his share of the business over to her and he refused, until a week after I opened Comfort & Joy and it was clear that we were doing well. That infuriated her. She finally got control of the restaurant and then worried that she'd be losing business to me."

"Did she? Have you taken business away from her?"

"She thought so, but I think there was plenty of room for both of us. She was still as busy as ever, from what I could tell."

Jake paused for a moment. He wasn't at all convinced that Jane had anything to do with this, regardless of how it looked. If she didn't, though, who did? What was he overlooking? He'd learned over the years that criminals almost always made at least one mistake and usually left something useful at the crime scene.

He walked over to the body again and stared at it intently, willing it to talk to him, to reveal its secrets. A cool breeze blew through and made the yellow sticky note flutter furiously. He leaned over and took a closer look at it. Then he looked back at Jane. "I took care of her for you. What do you suppose that means?"

"I don't know. But it seems like someone may have written that to make me look guilty."

"You think someone is trying to frame you? Why would anyone do that?"

"I honestly have no idea."

Jake scratched his head. "It's odd phrasing, though. It's almost as if someone wants you to know they did this for you. To impress you?" He chuckled then. "That doesn't make a whole lot of sense, though, does it?"

"Probably not," Janie agreed. But there was something in her tone that made him question her further.

"Is there anything at all that you're not telling me?"

"I don't think so. You're right, it's just too crazy. Impossible now. Though it is the kind of thing that I could have imagined Drummond doing, if he wasn't in jail."

"Alex Drummond? What's your connection to him?" Alex Drummond was a highly successful technology executive and a sadistic killer.

"He's the reason I moved home to Waverly."

3

Maybe we should go inside and sit a spell," Gramps suggested as the rest of Jake's team arrived. Jake excused himself for a moment to bring them up to speed, then followed them inside. Janie brought coffees for the three of them over to a small corner table, and then they sat and she filled Jake in on the reason why she'd moved home.

"I had a good job as a legal investigator at a large Boston law firm. I loved the work and I was good at it." She wasn't bragging, it was simply the truth. She was so good at her job that she helped the police catch one of the deadliest killers in years and almost lost her own life in the process.

"What exactly did you do?" Jake sounded curious about what her job had entailed.

"Ever watch The Good Wife? Know the character Kalinda?" she asked and he nodded. "That was me. I was usually able to get people to talk that wouldn't talk to anyone else.

Maybe I'm just less intimidating. And I'm good with computers."

That was an understatement. More than one person had said that Janie was gifted when it came to computers. She had a knack for hacking that was unexpected and had come in handy more than once.

"If you're that good with computers, why not work in the field?" Jake seemed confused by what her role had been.

Jane shrugged. "I'm easily bored, and I like variety. I still do the occasional consulting project, mostly security-related stuff. That job was a nice blend of everything. I enjoyed gathering information, reading people and solving the puzzle."

"Sounds like a career as a detective would make sense for you."

Jane frowned. "Too dangerous. As it turned out, the job at the law firm was also too dangerous. Once Drummond figured out that I was on to him, he was chasing me while I was trying to gather enough intel to catch him."

"So now you're happy baking pies and making coffee?" Jake sounded disbelieving.

"Happier than I've ever been. I love to cook and this has always been a dream, too. Just not something that I thought I'd do quite so soon. But, I'm glad that I did. I feel safe here. Or at least I did."

"Well, like you said, Drummond is behind bars, so that rules him out. Unfortunately, the only person who has any possible motive at the moment is you."

"Janie didn't do this," Gramps said.

Jake sighed. "I know. I don't think she did, either. I'm just saying that with our very limited information, she's the closest thing to a suspect that we have."

"How well do you know Samantha Sellers?" Jane asked. "There must be others who weren't fans of her."

"No doubt," Jake agreed. "I know she ruffled more than a few feathers over the years. There won't be any shortage of people to talk to." He took a final sip of coffee and then stood up.

"I should be getting back to the office now." He reached into his pocket and pulled something out of his wallet, then handed it to Jane. "Here's my card. If anything else comes to mind..." He hesitated for a moment and then added, "or if you talk to anyone and learn anything remotely interesting, please give me a call."

"I will, thank you."

As Jake walked out the back door, Jane heard Gramps chuckling softly.

"What's so funny?"

"Did you catch that? I think he just gave you the green light to start investigating—are you tempted?"

"Yes and no." The familiar instincts had already kicked in and Jane's mind was already spinning, going over what they already knew and trying to make sense of it. But at the same time, she could feel her chest muscles tighten, a sure sign that her stress level was increasing. If she gave in and started investigating again, she knew that somehow she would pay for it.

"Don't stress about it." Her grandfather knew her so well. "I'll help you!"

4

Jane ran some errands after closing the shop as usual at four in the afternoon. She unlocked her condo door with one hand while juggling two heavy grocery bags with the other. A minute after she walked through the door, her elderly Maine Coon cat, Misty, came sauntering down the hallway to greet her. Misty moved like a confident lion, as if she was king of the mountain instead of a six-pound ball of fur.

Jane scooped her up and gave her a quick hug before she wiggled out of her arms and demanded, quite loudly, to be fed. It was their usual routine. She rummaged through one of the grocery bags for her food, opened a can and dumped it into a small bowl. Then, she poured herself half a glass of white wine and stepped out onto her deck.

What a day it had been. Just when she thought she'd put everything behind her, something like this happened. Waverly rarely had murders. The last one had been a few years ago, when a student went missing and was then found dead. Like most murders, he was killed by someone he knew. Her cousin David's wife, Lauren, had been his teacher.

The biggest issue Waverly generally had was an occasional heroin overdose. The problem was growing, even in the smallest towns. But, Gramps was proud of the fact that so far, none of the overdoses had resulted in a death, thanks to the fact that all local police and emergency responders carried Narcan pens, which were a powerful antidote.

For the most part, though, Waverly was a quiet, quaint seaside town. The kind of place where anytime you go to the grocery store or shopping along Main Street, you were likely to run into people you know.

Jane had always loved it, but hadn't been around much in recent years, since her mother remarried. The only family she had left in the area was Gramps and her cousin David. She had no siblings and her father had been gone now for just over ten years.

She'd been lucky to find this condo so quickly. That was thanks to Gramps. He lived a few doors down and had called her the minute the rental went on the market. He'd only just moved in himself a year before, looking to downsize from the larger home he'd lived in for over fifty years.

His condo was a different layout from hers. It was one level so he didn't have to deal with the stairs. Hers was three levels if you included the finished basement. Her favorite feature was the deck that looked out over the ocean. They were close enough to have a pretty view, but high up on a hill so flooding would never be an issue.

The breeze ruffled her hair as she sipped her wine and

tried to calm her racing thoughts. She thought that she'd put investigating behind her, yet here she was with a dead body and a lot of unanswered questions. It was both terrifying and tempting at the same time. If nothing else, she wanted to help find them someone else to focus on. Jake might be kind enough to dismiss her as a suspect, but if no one else emerged, attention would likely fall on her again, and she didn't need that.

She jumped as the phone suddenly rang, snapping her out of her thoughts. She smiled as the caller ID said it was her mother.

"Hi, Mom."

There was a crackle of static in the background and then her mother's voice came through. "Hi, honey. We just docked in Bali and came ashore, so I wanted to let you know where we are. Reception isn't great here. How are you?" Her mother's new husband, Jim, was a semi-retired executive who was also an obsessive sailor. They had been at sea for several months now, making their way slowly around the world.

"I'm good. Well, actually I've been better." Jane filled her mother in on the day's events.

"Oh, no, how awful. That poor woman. I never did like her much, but still I wouldn't wish her ill. How are you doing with it all? I hope you're not planning to get involved?"

Jane said nothing.

"Really, Janie, that wouldn't be a good idea. Let the professionals do their job. Stay out of the way and focus on your shop. Do what makes you happy."

"I'm trying to do that, Mom." Her mother seemed satisfied with that answer.

"Good. So, let me tell you what we've been up to...." After about thirty minutes of her mother's travel monologue, which was the usual chatter about all the interesting people they were meeting and different types of food they were trying, they finally hung up and Jane reached for the sweater she'd brought with her and pulled it on. The air was getting cooler and the sun was almost gone as the dark of night rolled in.

With regret, Jane decided that it was probably best to head inside for the evening. She stood and shivered again from the cold and from her mother's last words—"Honey, don't forget to lock all your doors. Waverly seems like the safest place in the world, but you can never be too careful."

5

The next morning at around ten thirty, the morning rush was over and the only people left in the store were Gramps and his two buddies, who were just getting up to leave as well. Jane asked Melissa to keep an eye on things for a little bit while she ran out to run an errand. She untied her apron, grabbed her purse and headed for the front door. Gramps held it open for her. "Where are you off to in such a hurry?"

"I thought I'd take a walk down to the Sellers' bed and breakfast and see if Chester is around. Pay my condolences, maybe ask a few questions."

"I'm coming with you." It wasn't a question, and truthfully, Jane was happy to have Gramps' company. She'd never been fond of Samantha's soon to be ex-husband, Chester, and didn't relish the thought of walking into his restaurant alone.

"Wonderful, let's go." They walked the short distance to

the other restaurant. Like her shop, it was a slow time for them, too, and the only person there was Chester, who was leaning behind the front counter, where all the to-go muffins and bagels were kept. He was reading the Boston Herald and stirring sugar into what looked like a freshly poured cup of coffee. He looked up in curiosity and then surprise when he saw Jane and Gramps walk in.

"Morning. What brings the two of you in?"

"I heard your banana nut muffins are better than mine, so I wanted to find out for myself," Jane said with a smile. "I also wanted to offer my condolences. I'm very sorry for your loss."

"I'm very sorry as well," Gramps added.

"Thank you, both. Two muffins, then?" he asked as he opened a small paper bag and slid on a plastic glove to handle the food.

"Why not?" Gramps agreed.

"How are you doing?" Jane asked sympathetically, hoping to draw him out.

Chester dropped the second muffin in the bag, folded the top down and then handed it to her.

"Anything else?" he asked, seemingly ignoring her question.

"No, thanks."

She handed him a ten-dollar bill and as he rang it through the register he said, "It's a bit surreal to me. The day before yesterday we were screaming at each other, another huge fight about who gets what and then, just like that, she's gone."

He handed her the change and added, "It's kind of strange, actually. I'd finally agreed to give her my share of the business, and now the whole thing is mine. I'm not even sure that I want it."

"Have you been working together all along?" Jane asked, curious about their volatile dynamic.

"Off and on, mostly off." He smiled and then explained, "The place seems to run better when only one of us is in charge. I've been gone for over a month now while we worked this out, and didn't have any plans to come back."

"Did you go away somewhere?"

"What?" He seemed distracted by the question at first. "Oh, no. I've mostly been here, just focusing on other things."

"What else do you do?" He was a big man, and Jane noticed that his hands were rough and calloused.

"I run a small construction business, mostly kitchen and bath remodeling. That's my main interest."

"Do you have any thoughts on what happened to your wife?" Gramps asked.

"Ex-wife. Or at least she was soon to be. I guess she is now, though, isn't she?" He chuckled nervously and then said, "I don't have any idea what happened to her. She drove me crazy, and more than once I wanted to kill her, but I could never actually do it." He chuckled again, and added, "I suppose that doesn't sound very good, does it?"

Jane's first instinct was to tell him that she understood, but instead, she simply smiled and said, "I hope they find out who did this soon." She put her change back in her purse and picked up the bag of muffins.

"We'll leave you to it, then," Gramps said as they walked toward the door.

"What do you make of him?" Jane asked Gramps as they walked back toward her shop. She reached into the paper bag and broke a piece off one of the muffins. She popped it in her mouth, and then sighed. They really were good. Not better than hers, of course, but close, very close.

"Pass that bag over here," Gramps demanded. Once he helped himself to a chunk of muffin, he considered her question.

"I don't think he did it. No real reason to. He was almost rid of her."

Jane thought about that for a moment. "That's true, but now he doesn't have to give away half of what he owned. The restaurant is his again. Everything is his."

"That's true. Still, my gut says he didn't do it."

"Has your gut ever been wrong?" Jane was curious. Her grandfather had been very good at his job—exceptional, even.

"My gut has fooled me a few times over the years, I'll admit that. My track record is pretty good, but you never do know for sure."

"You know her much better than I do. Can you think of anyone who would benefit from her death?"

Gramps reached for the muffin bag again before answering.

"She wasn't a popular woman. In recent years, she was even more difficult, burned a lot of bridges. I know her stepsister wasn't her biggest fan. Rumor is she was having an affair with a local lawyer in town, a married lawyer. Don't know of anyone that had a motive, though, other than just not liking the woman. That's usually not enough."

"No, you're right. We need to keep digging. Sounds like there's no shortage of people to talk to."

"Every conversation leads to something else," Gramps said as they reached the front door of Comfort & Joy.

Jane paused before saying, "Mom doesn't want me to get involved."

"I love your mother, but she doesn't understand what we do. She never did. How is she?"

"She's good. Just landed in Bali. You'll probably hear from her soon." Jane opened the front door and then turned back to Gramps. "Thing is, though, she does have a point. I was supposed to be walking away from investigating."

"Good luck with that, Janie," Gramps said with a grin.

6

Except for Melissa, who was taking a tray of steaming chicken pot pies out of the oven, Comfort & Joy was completely empty when Jane returned. She had left her cellphone on the kitchen counter and saw that she'd missed a call from her ex-boyfriend, Nick. They had parted on amicable, yet strained, terms. Nick wanted to try to work things out, but Jane didn't see the point. They were too different and it had been going on for too long.

Nick was a senior partner at the law firm she'd worked at in Boston. She'd found that impressive, at first. With his thick, blond hair and tall, athletic build, he was a very attractive man, and she'd also been drawn to his charisma and intellect.

Nick was a very smart and powerful man. He was also power-driven and work-obsessed. He lived and breathed the law firm. After a while, it got old and even when she was dealing with the craziness that was Alex Drummond, Nick had offered little comfort. He was simply too busy.

He'd left a voice message, short and to the point—typical Nick. He wanted her to call him immediately. She really didn't feel like talking to him, but it was a good time to call back, before the shop got busy again. And, she was curious about his reason for calling. Nick had never been the type to call with no reason.

He answered on the second ring. "Nick Tanner." His tone was clipped; he was clearly in the middle of a million things.

"It's Jane."

His tone softened. "I'm sorry, I didn't even look at the caller ID. It's crazy here. You know how it is."

Jane could picture him behind his desk in his massive, corner office with the breathtaking view of Boston Harbor that he was too busy to enjoy. "I do, indeed. You called?"

"We should meet for lunch this week." Typical Nick. Her shop was at its busiest during the lunch hour. Going out to lunch herself was next to impossible.

"It's hard for me to get out during the day. The shop closes at four, though. I could meet you after that, or we could just talk on the phone. What's going on?" She knew Nick well enough to know this wasn't a social invitation. Neither one of them was still pining for the other.

Nick hesitated. "I miss seeing you, and bouncing ideas off of you. We always worked well together."

Was that his angle? To try and get her to come back? She thought she'd been clear with everyone there that that wasn't going to happen. "I could save you the trip, Nick. I'm not coming back."

"No, of course you're not. Like I said, I just want to bounce something off you. I value your opinion. And I want to make sure you're really all right."

Jane smiled. Deep down, he really was a good guy—just not the best boyfriend. "Why don't we meet after work? I can come into the city and we can have a drink somewhere?"

"You don't mind? I could come to you."

"I don't mind. It's been a while since I've been to the Back Bay."

"How about tomorrow, then, at six, at the Oak Room?"

"Perfect, see you then."

7

Jane took the T into the city the following day. She normally preferred to drive but wasn't keen on sitting in rush hour traffic, which started getting heavy by three on most days. She took the orange line into the Back Bay area of Boston. She exited the subway and came up the steps and onto the hustle and bustle of Boylston Street, and at that moment, she missed the energy of the city.

People were streaming down the stairs to the trains and walking along the busy street. Boylston Street in Copley Square had always been one of her favorite areas. It was pretty and historic, with the grand old Trinity stone church in the middle of the square, with the public library nearby and excellent boutiques and restaurants everywhere.

Right in the heart of Copley Square was the Fairmont Hotel and its luxurious Oak Bar. It was Nick's favorite place for a drink after work or to meet with potential new clients and was just a block from her old office. As Jane stepped inside, she could see Nick at the far end of the bar, checking messages on his phone. She made her way over to him, admiring as she often did, the dark polished wood everywhere, and when she slid into the seat next to Nick, she relaxed into the soft, buttery leather.

"Great to see you." Nick leaned in to give her a hug. "Nuts?"

He slid the silver bowl of mixed nuts her way. She reached for a few. The hot, salty nuts at the Oak Bar were another reason she liked it there. Nick had a barely touched the scotch on the rocks in front of him and when the bartender came their way, Jane ordered a chardonnay.

"So, how are you really, Jane? You look good."

That was nice to hear. Jane had tried on a few different things before settling on the dusty rose cashmere sweater and charcoal gray pants. She wasn't trying to impress Nick, but the faded jeans and powder pink Life Is Good tee-shirt she wore at the shop all day wouldn't have been appropriate. Especially when he looked as good as she knew he would.

Nick had great hair, thick and blond and just a hint of gel so it looked slightly tousled, and he wore a suit really well. Today's was deep navy with a steel gray tie. Elegant and powerful. She felt a hint of the old attraction but willed it to go away.

"The shop is doing well, better than expected," she told him, and then took a sip of her wine. It was smooth and buttery with just a hint of oak. A perfect chardonnay.

"I'm glad the shop is doing well, but what about you? Are you really happy just cooking all day?" The look on his face was priceless. Cooking was apparently on a par with taking out the garbage to Nick—impossible for him to imagine anyone liking the work.

Jane smiled. "I'm happier than I've been in a long time, and much more relaxed. Cooking suits me. Being back in Waverly is good for me. Even after what happened yesterday."

She figured he had to know about the murder. Coverage had been all over the news. Though they'd left out the part about the sticky note. Gramps had explained that was the kind of detail the police generally withheld from the public, at least initially.

"What happened yesterday?" So he didn't know about the murder.

"You don't watch the news anymore?" she teased him.

He laughed a bit. "I was up until two working on a case. Missed it."

She told him about Samantha Sellers. A funny expression crossed his face when she got to the part about the sticky note.

"What did it say again?" he asked.

"I took care of her for you."

Nick took another sip of his scotch. "That's interesting."

"I think it's downright strange." It still didn't make any sense to Jane at all.

"Well, it's just odd, considering." Nick paused for a moment. "The reason I wanted to see you is to discuss a somewhat troubling situation. Alex Drummond has been asking for you."

Jane shivered and reached for her glass, for something to hold on to.

"Why is he asking for me? What does he want?"

"That's the strange part. I don't really know. I received a request to meet with him a few days ago. So I went, reluctantly, but admittedly I was curious. He was actually very complimentary about you."

"What?" The thought of it was almost creepier than his anger.

Alex Drummond was actually a very handsome man and almost hypnotically charismatic. His mood could change on a dime, though, and Jane had seen the shift happen, when it was almost as if someone waved their hand across his face and he went from charm to intense anger in a flash. It was unsettling.

"He said he'd had a lot of time to think about things recently and he realized that he'd underestimated you. He said that he admires your intellect."

Jane squirmed in her seat. "And I'm supposed to care about this because…"

"He wants to meet with you. That was the whole reason he brought me in there, so I could persuade you to see him. I agreed to pass on his message, but I told him it was doubtful that you'd agree."

"I don't want to meet with him," she said automatically. It was a reflex action. Every cell in her body screamed that it was a bad idea.

"I don't blame you. I wouldn't want to, either. You certainly don't have to."

"I've been having the nightmares again," she admitted.

"I'm sorry to hear that. All the more reason not to go

there." Nick reached for the nuts and popped a cashew in his mouth.

"Why do you think he wants to meet with me?" That was the puzzling thing. What could he possibly want with her?

"He didn't say. I asked twice, but he danced around the question both times. Just said he thought you were an exceptional young lady. It was definitely odd."

"Well, I can't think of any good reason to go. I don't want to dredge all that up again."

"I don't blame you a bit. I'll send a message letting him know."

"So, how is everyone else in the office doing? Fill me in."

There were a few people that Jane had really enjoyed working with. It was a friendly, tight-knit office and was a work hard, play hard environment. They had often gone for drinks after a long day, and at times Jane did miss that camaraderie.

"Well, Ellie just got engaged…" For the next hour, Nick caught her up on all the office, gossip and when the bartender noticed her empty glass and asked if she wanted another, she regretfully declined.

"I'd love to stay longer, but I get up really early these days."

"That's right. It will be soon be time to make the donuts," he teased, referencing the infamous Dunkin' Donuts commercial.

"It was good seeing you, Nick." And it was. She was glad that they were all doing well.

Nick put his hand over hers and smiled. It was the look that used to make her melt.

"I've missed you. Let's do this again soon."

If she wanted to, she could be right back where was with Nick before, Jane realized. The old attraction was obviously still there for him, too. But if she went there, things would just be the same as they were before, and she was quite sure she didn't want that. No matter how hot and charming he was.

"Have a good night, Nick."

8

A week later, Jake was no closer to finding Samantha Sellers' killer. It was Friday morning, a little past nine, and he'd been in the office since six, poring over everything they'd gathered so far. But their evidence folder was thin, very thin. There was no real evidence. The fingerprinting and DNA testing had turned up nothing—which in itself was a bit interesting. It was an extremely clean crime scene.

Whoever had killed Samantha Sellers had either done this before and knew what they were doing, or they were just an impressively prepared beginner, perhaps one with OCD tendencies, because the body and the crime scene were spotless. There wasn't a single fingerprint anywhere, and the one stray hair they'd found and sent off for DNA testing had belonged to the victim.

Jake had spoken to everyone he could think of who knew the victim—family, friends, enemies. There were plenty of people who didn't like Samantha. A few even could be considered to have something of a motive for murder, but even then, nothing further was turning up.

There had only been one murder on his watch, and he'd been able to solve it. This one shouldn't present such difficulties. On the surface, it seemed simple enough. But he knew from years of experience that things were often very different from how they originally appeared. The truth was out there; he just hadn't dug deep enough. He would find it, though. He always did.

He stood up and stretched. His back was already getting stiff from sitting in the same position too long, hunched over his computer. His stomach rumbled and he remembered that he didn't stop for his usual bagel on the way in, as it was too early. Maybe he'd run up to Janie Cho's place and grab a muffin and another cup of coffee. He wouldn't mind seeing Janie again and if he was going to start questioning everyone again, he might as well start with her.

Besides, he couldn't officially rule Janie off his potential list of suspects, because she did have both motive and opportunity, given that the body was found at her shop. But, the autopsy results showed that the victim had been killed several hours earlier, which would put the time of death around six a.m. when both of them were starting their days.

Janie would have already been at the shop by then, getting ready to open at seven. Could she have really gone to Samantha's place, killed her and moved the body all by herself? That wasn't likely. Samantha was several inches taller and at least thirty pounds heavier than Jane. Even a body the same size or smaller would have been a challenge for her, as there was a reason for the expression, 'dead weight'. It wasn't easy to move a dead body.

The only other possibility, if he was seriously considering Janie as a suspect, would be if she had somehow lured Samantha to come to Comfort & Joy and then killed her. That way, she wouldn't have to move the body. But still, it didn't really add up. If she did it, why would she leave that cryptic note which only served to tie her into the murder in some way? Though he wouldn't stop investigating everyone, including Janie, should additional information come his way, non-officially, Jake had ruled her out.

But, he did want to talk to her again, and to run an idea by her.

9

There was a small line when Jake arrived at Comfort &
Joy, but it moved along quickly. He couldn't help but
admire Janie as she worked, taking orders and chatting with
the customers. She seemed to know them all by name, which
meant they were likely regulars. In a short time, she seemed
to be building a good business and a loyal clientele. Jake was
impressed. When he reached the register, Janie had an au-
tomatic smile for him, which turned to surprise when she
recognized him.

"Good morning, Jake. Nice to see you again. What can I
get for you?" There was no one waiting behind him, so Jake
hoped that she might have a few minutes to talk to him.

"I'll take an onion bagel with cream cheese and a small
black coffee, please."

"Is that to go? Or for here?"

"I'll have it here."

Janie filled a cranberry-colored ceramic mug with coffee

and slid it towards him. "If you'd like to have a seat, I'll bring that over to you when it's ready," she said.

Jake settled himself at a small table against the wall and glanced around the room while he waited. It was a quarter to ten now, so the place wasn't as busy as he'd imagined it was earlier. Two young mothers sat sipping lattes in the corner, with their strollers by their sides. There was only one other table of customers.

"Morning, Jake," Gramps called over to him. Janie's grandfather was sitting with two of his friends at the center table. Holding court, it looked like, as they'd been chatting with some of the other regulars when Jake had walked in. Their plates were empty, but they were still sipping coffee and Jake guessed they were in no hurry to go anywhere. Jake stood and walked over to say hello.

"Hi, Gramps, Carl, and Eddie. How are you all?" At ninety-two, Gramps was the most senior of the three, but you'd never know it. He still had the energy and sharpness of a much younger man. Jake's best friend, David, was very close to his grandfather and because of it, Jake had spent a good amount of time with him as well over the years. He had been a key influence in his decision to go into police work.

"Can't complain. Just had the best blueberry muffin known to man. You tried one of Janie's muffins yet?"

Jake chuckled. "Not yet, but I have a bagel coming."

"Well, one of these mornings, get the blueberry muffin. You won't regret it." His smile faded as his tone turned more serious. "How's the investigation going? Any luck finding out who killed Samantha Sellers?"

"Not yet. We will figure it out, though," he promised.

"You might want to see if Janie can help," Gramps suggested with a sly smile. "Once you clear her as a suspect, of course."

"What?" Jake wasn't sure he'd heard correctly.

"There she is, just ask her."

Jake walked back to his table, where Janie was setting down a buttered bagel and a side of cream cheese.

"Here you go," she said.

"Thanks. Do you have a minute to talk?"

Janie looked around the restaurant, which was practically empty now except for Gramps and his buddies. The only other customers, the two young mothers, were wheeling their strollers out the front door.

"Sure, I can sit for a bit." She pulled out a chair and sat across from him at the small table. Jake sat as well and reached for the cream cheese, spreading it on his bagel as he spoke.

"Your grandfather said I should ask you for your help. What did he mean by that?"

"He shouldn't have said that." She spoke quickly and glanced over at her grandfather, who was beaming back at the both of them.

Jake decided to drop that for the time being and to ask his questions. "We haven't come up with anything promising. No real leads yet, though I'm continuing to talk to people and to circle back to the ones I've spoken with to see if there's anything else they can think of that might be relevant, that they forgot to mention the first time we spoke. So, that's why I'm here today, besides the fact that I forgot my breakfast on the way in," he added with a grin.

"You want to know if I remember anything else? Or if

anything else has happened?" Janie asked.

That caught Jake's attention. He hadn't quite asked that, and something had obviously happened. He just nodded and waited for her to continue.

"I don't remember anything else. It really was as simple as it seemed. When I took out the trash, there she was. I have no idea how long she was there. It must have been long before I arrived that morning, I would imagine?"

"Autopsy results suggested that she was there for several hours before you found her," he confirmed.

"It's just the strangest thing. The door to the shed was unlocked, too. I'm nearly a hundred percent certain that I locked that door the night before. I always lock it."

"Where do you keep the key?"

"In the kitchen, on a hook by the back door."

Jake thought for a moment. "So whoever used that key had to come into the store to get it?"

"Yes, and the thought of that is a bit unsettling. There's no sign of forced entry."

"You're sure?"

Janie shot him a scornful look. "Yes, I'm sure, but would you like to take a look?"

"Yes, if you don't mind. Though I'm sure you're right on that." He smiled at her and her look of irritation faded away. "I'm pretty sure the team checked both front and back doors when they were here, but it never hurts to have another look." He took a big bite of his bagel and then stood up, and Janie led him through the kitchen to the back door. He opened it and jiggled the lock back and forth.

"Looks untouched to me," he said.

"Like I said, it's the strangest thing."

Janie followed him back to his table and once they were settled again, he turned his attention back to his bagel for a moment and then casually asked, "So, was there something else that happened?"

Janie hesitated as if she was debating what to say or how much to share. He noticed her clear eyes cloud over. Something was definitely troubling her.

"Gramps and I took a walk down the road to the Sellers' bed and breakfast and chatted with Chester, Samantha's husband."

"Oh, are you friendly with him?" He'd heard that Samantha was no fan of Janie's so thought it was interesting that they'd visit her husband.

"Friendly with Chester? No. I hardly know the man. We thought it would be a good idea to talk to him to see if he might make sense as a suspect."

"You went there to investigate him?" Jake was surprised.

"Yes. The sooner you figure out who killed Samantha Sellers, the sooner my life gets back to normal. I like normal."

Jake took another bite of his bagel and pushed away his sense of irritation that Janie was interfering with his investigation. In spite of himself, he couldn't help asking, "So, did you learn anything?"

"Well, there's no love lost between the two of them. Chester was looking forward to finalizing the divorce. He said the two of them couldn't work together at all anymore."

"So, do you think that gives him a motive?" Jake had talked to Chester, too, and was curious to hear Janie's impression of him.

Janie sighed. "Technically, I suppose it does. Now everything is his. But I really don't think he did it. He seemed more than happy to give her the bed and breakfast and focus his attention elsewhere. He has a construction company. I think the restaurant was more her baby than his."

"That's what I thought as well when I talked to him, and it seems like he may have an alibi. His sister said that he stayed at her house that night. He was doing some work for her and then had dinner and drinks and didn't want to drive."

Janie fiddled with a napkin on the table and looked as though she still had something that she was debating sharing.

"So, was that what your grandfather was referring to? When he said I should ask for your help?"

Janie sighed. "Probably. He thinks it would be good for me to help investigate. I'm not so sure I agree with him."

"Why's that?" Jake was curious. She didn't seem at all eager to get involved.

"I put all that behind me when I left the law firm. Or at least I thought I did." She bit her lower lip and glanced around the room.

"What is it?"

"I had a strange phone call yesterday, from someone I used to work with. I went to meet up with him for a drink last night. You're familiar with the Alex Drummond case?"

Jake nodded and said, "That tech executive who was convicted of three murders?"

"Yes. We were defending one of his employees, who was initially implicated in the murders. I was the lead investigator for the defense. What we uncovered didn't bode well for Mr. Drummond."

"Your client got off completely, if I recall?"

"Yes, he was totally innocent. Drummond had done a clever job of framing him and he almost got away with it."

"So, how does this involve you now? Has there been a new development with his case or appeal? He is appealing, I assume."

"Yes, he's appealing. I don't think he has anything that will help him, though." Janie paused then and then continued. "He tried to kill me while I was doing the investigation. Not him personally, but someone he hired. I'm lucky to be alive. It's the reason why I left the law firm and why I had nightmares for months after, until he was finally convicted."

"So, that's why you're here?" Jake understood, more than she realized. It was why he'd left Boston as well, to take a post in Waverly where the pace was different. He'd burned out in Boston, working homicide and being involved in one murder case after another. It took a toll on him. Though as dangerous as the work was, he'd never come as close to being killed as Janie had.

"Yes, it's why I'm here. I miss the work at times, but not enough to go back. I thought that's what Nick wanted to talk about at first. Either that or us getting back together." She smiled at that and then laughed nervously. "It wasn't either of those things, though. Nick had been summoned to see Drummond and he asked Nick to arrange a meeting with me."

"He wants to meet with you? I hope you said no." Jake

tensed at the idea, feeling protective on Janie's behalf. He wouldn't want anyone that he knew to be too close to a monster like that.

"I did. I wasn't too keen on the idea myself."

"Do you have any idea why he wanted to meet with you?"

"None at all. And I have to admit, I'm curious. But not enough to go meet with him. I just don't think I'm ready for that. I'm not sure if I ever will be. It's kind of funny, though. My nightmares started up again about a week ago."

"Really? That is odd." Jake found it interesting, too. It made him wonder if there was something she knew, or at least her subconscious did.

"So you can understand why I'm hesitant to get involved, as tempting as it is?" Janie asked as she stood up to head back to the kitchen.

"I do. If you do decide to scratch that itch and ask around some, keep me posted. I'll check in again next week."

Janie smiled. "Well, when you do, I look forward to hearing what you've discovered."

10

Gramps and his buddies were getting ready to leave as Janie walked back towards the kitchen.

"You to go on ahead. I need to talk to Janie," Gramps said as she reached their table.

Gramps was still seated, so Jane pulled out a chair and joined him.

"Where are you off to today?" she asked. Her grandfather had a much busier social life than she did, it seemed.

"Going to head home for a little bit now, check on the cats." When her grandmother passed a few years back, Gramps had a rough first year and decided to adopt two kittens. He'd quickly grown to love the companionship of Moe and Larry and they'd helped add life to a painfully empty home.

"The bereavement group meets at three and then we'll probably be going out to dinner at the 99 after, like we usually do."

Janie smiled. The bereavement group had been a godsend

for Gramps. He'd resisted going at first. The idea of sitting around talking to other people who had recently lost loved ones seemed depressing and intimidating, even. But he went, and once he got to know the people, he found that it helped so much to talk about how he was feeling.

Most people stayed in groups like that for a short while, but Gramps helped turn it into more of a social group, and once they all felt better, they started making a routine of going out to an early dinner after the meeting. Janie had once asked him why he kept going and he'd said that now that he was better, he could help make the new people who joined feel welcome and let them know that he'd gone through a similar struggle.

"Is Judy going?" Gramps had recently become friendly with one of the women in the group and they'd gone out a few times, though Gramps was always quick to say they were just friends. He seemed to have a lot of women friends.

He frowned for a moment. "They'll both be there, most likely. The good Judy and the bad Judy."

"Oh, that's right. I forgot about the bad Judy." There were two women in the bereavement group both named Judy. The good Judy was the one Gramps enjoyed spending time with. Jane had met her and she was a lovely woman. The other Judy, the bad Judy, Jane hadn't met. She had a somewhat aggressive interest in her grandfather and he found it off-putting.

"Did I tell you she showed up at my house two nights ago? Had a casserole for me. She wanted to come in and visit but I told her I was on my way out. I think she'd been drinking."

"What kind of casserole was it?" Her grandfather would

usually eat just about anything, especially if it was covered in cheese.

"I have no idea. I couldn't identify anything in it and I didn't like the smell of it. The bad Judy really isn't a very good cook. Moe and Larry wouldn't even touch it."

Jane laughed at that. "Well, tell the good Judy I said hello."

"I'll do that. So, what did Jake have to tell you?" Gramps finally got to the real reason why he wanted to stay and talk to her.

"Not much. I think he was just circling back to question me again. He seemed surprised that you suggested to him that I help investigate."

"If he knew you, he would think it's a good idea, too," Gramps said.

"He didn't seem too opposed to the idea. I could tell he was a little wary at first, but then he seemed to warm up to it, and I think he'd welcome the help, actually. So far, they've up come with nothing."

"We need to make a list. Everyone Jake's already talked to and anyone else we can think of who might have an issue with Samantha."

"That might be a long list." Jane had been thinking the same thing though.

"I'll work on my list tonight, and we can compare notes in the morning and then divvy them up." Gramps was enthusiastic about their project and Jane admired his energy. She had been debating whether or not to share her other news with Gramps. She didn't want to alarm him needlessly, but she also valued his opinion and knew he'd be furious if she didn't tell him.

"I had a call from Nick yesterday."

"Nick from Boston? The one you used to go with?"

"Yes, and work with. I went to see him after work. Drummond called him in for a meeting."

"What did he want?" Gramps already looked angry, and when she told him that Drummond wanted to meet with her, he looked like he wanted to explode.

"What does he want with you?"

"I don't know. I have no idea. I told Nick to tell him no, of course. Still, I thought it was strange."

Gramps paced back and forth for a moment and then finally stopped and faced Jane.

"I think you should see him."

"What? You do?" Jane was truly shocked. She had expected his anger on her behalf, but had also assumed he'd agree with her and insist that she stay clear of Drummond.

"I do. See what the man wants, and get some closure for yourself. Make the nightmares stop."

"What if seeing him makes them worse?" That was her biggest fear.

"How could it be worse than not knowing? Aren't you curious to know why he wants to see you?"

Gramps knew her so well. She'd been wondering about it all day and hadn't slept well at all the night before.

"You're right, as usual. I'll go see him."

"Do you want me to go with you?" Gramps stood up straight, ready to protect her and it made her want to give him a hug.

"No, thank you. I think it's best that I go alone."

11

Jane knew she'd made the right decision. On the way home from work, she felt a sense of relief that then shifted into apprehension. As Gramps had said, she was curious about what Drummond wanted from her and it had been eating at her all day. She couldn't imagine why he would even give her another thought, now that the case was over and especially since he obviously knew that she'd left her job at the law firm. He had nothing left to fear from her.

When she got home, she quickly fed Misty and then jumped in the shower. She was heading to David and Lauren's house for dinner and needed to pick up a bottle of wine along the way as well. An hour later, she was dressed and out the door. She brought a bottle of merlot, since Lauren was making her famous spaghetti and meatballs.

Jane had always been close with her cousin David and she adored his wife, Lauren, who was a high school teacher in Waverly. They'd only been married for about a year and they'd both been incredibly supportive when Jane first moved to Waverly and was settling in.

Lauren had been especially sympathetic, as she'd dealt with a difficult situation herself in the weeks before her marriage. One of her students had gone missing and when he was found dead soon after, Lauren became a person of interest in his murder. But, they finally caught the true murderer and Lauren's name was cleared.

Lauren was in the kitchen tossing a salad when she arrived, and David took the bottle of wine and went in search of an opener.

"I'm so glad we decided to do this. I haven't seen you in ages," Lauren said as she came over to give Jane a hello hug.

"I know. These past few weeks have been crazy," Jane said as she shrugged her jacket off and hung it in the front closet.

"How is the store doing?" David asked as he handed her a glass of wine. Jane settled onto one of the high-backed stools that lined the island Lauren was working at.

"It's busy. Seems to be growing each week."

"That's great! I'll have to try and stop by on my way to work. I keep meaning to," Lauren said apologetically.

"I'll remind her. Once she tries one of your muffins you won't be able to keep her away," David chuckled.

"You sound like Gramps," Jane said.

David settled in the chair next to her and grabbed a slice of cheese from a plate of cheese and crackers.

"I heard you talked to Jake earlier," he said casually.

Jane was surprised. "How did you know that?"

"I called him on my way home from work, to confirm our plans to watch the game tomorrow night and we got to talking. He asked me about you."

"What do you mean?" Jane felt excited for a moment then realized he was probably referring to her former job.

"He wanted to know how good you were. At investigating. I told him you were the best and he'd be lucky if you ever gave him any help at all. I think that satisfied him."

"Did he mention anything else?" She wondered exactly how much Jake had shared with David.

"You mean about Drummond?" Crap. She couldn't help but feel annoyed that he'd told David that.

"Don't be mad. I can tell by your face that you're pissed. He's just worried for you and figured I'd want to know. He knows me well."

"I would have told you anyway," she admitted.

"So, you have no idea what he wants?" David leaned forward and tapped his fingers back and forth on the counter, a habit Jane recognized as something that he did when he was trying to figure out a problem.

"None."

"Are you sure you want to meet with him? I don't know if I'd be able to. He looks pretty intimidating on TV. I don't think I'd want to get that close," Lauren said.

"I don't want to meet with him, not at all. But, I can't not do it, if that makes sense. I need to know what he wants. So I can deal with it, and move on, for good."

"Will anyone be with you? Gramps said he offered."

"You talked to Gramps, too? When?"

"He called me at work and said he was on his way to his bereavement group. He's just worried about you. I think he felt a little guilty for suggesting it."

Jane sighed. "I'm not going because of Gramps, although he did surprise me. I didn't think he'd want me to go near Drummond. But, he knows me so well. Knows the curiosity would be too much. He's right."

"And what about Samantha Sellers? Gramps mentioned that you're going to investigate that together? Do you know if anyone has talked to Maxine Cummings?"

"Maxine Cummings? Who is that?" Even though Jane had grown up in Waverly, there were still so many unfamiliar people.

"Samantha's stepsister. They barely spoke. Maybe it was worse than anyone knew?"

"I'm sure Jake must have talked to her, but we will, too. Did anyone like that woman?"

"Samantha? The only person she seemed friendly with was Ellen Smith. They were best friends," Lauren said as she spread a mix of soft butter, garlic and chopped parsley across two halves of a loaf of Italian bread.

"She's friendly with Ellen? Really?" Ellen Smith was also a high school teacher and had recently become a regular at Comfort & Joy, stopping in most mornings on her way to work for a coffee to go.

"I wonder if Samantha knew she'd started coming to my place."

"If she did, I don't think they'd be on very good terms." Lauren laughed as she slid the buttered bread into the oven to bake.

"I will have a chat with Ellen next time she comes in." Jane was curious to know if Ellen and Samantha may have had a falling out. Either that or she was keeping her morning coffee routine a secret. It would be interesting to find out.

"So, if Gramps isn't going in with you, who will? Will Nick be there?" David clearly didn't like the idea of Jane facing Drummond alone. Jane wasn't too keen on it, either. But, she knew it was for the best if they had any hope of getting any information.

"Nick is going with me, but we both agreed that it's best for me to actually meet with Drummond alone. He'll be behind glass, so I'll be perfectly safe."

David frowned. "Why is it better for you to be alone? I don't like it."

"Nick will be there, right outside the door. But, Drummond asked to meet just with me. We figured there's a reason for that, that he might be more open."

"I suppose that makes sense. As long as Nick is nearby"

"How is Nick? Any chance the two of you might work things out?" Lauren looked hopeful. She'd always liked Nick. Everyone liked Nick, though. He was quite likable, just not great boyfriend material.

"I don't think so, but I think we can work on being friends."

Lauren looked disappointed. "That's something, then. So, are we ready to eat?"

12

Jane felt a mix of nerves and curiosity when Nick pulled into the lot at the state jail in Plymouth. This is where a lot of the high profile cases were sent until further determination was made on where to send them. Plymouth was a large but sleepy town on Boston's South Shore. Most of the inmates were here for minor offenses, except for the maximum security wing, where Alex Drummond was residing. Jane's shoes were loud as they walked down the silent hallways and then finally reached the waiting area. She checked in at the reception desk, showed her ID and then took a seat. Nick sat next to her.

"You can still change your mind. You don't have to meet with him." Nick seemed almost more nervous than she was, if that was possible. Jane took a deep breath. The thought had crossed her mind. Just say no and walk away.

"No, I want to. I do."

Twenty minutes later, a correctional officer stepped into

the waiting area and called her name. Jane stood.

"Follow me."

Nick stood, too. "You sure you don't want me to come with you?"

"I do, you know I do. But I have to go alone."

"I'll be right here." Nick sat back down and Jane followed the guard out of the room and down an endless hall. Finally, she was led into a visiting room that had a wall of Plexiglas separating a long desk and phones on either side. Drummond was sitting there waiting. He was tall, easily six foot three or even six four, and rangy with longish, sandy blond hair and whisker shadows along his chin. He was a handsome man, but as he smiled at her, a sly smile that he no doubt thought was charming, all Jane could focus on was his eyes. They were dead and cold. Chilling. She took a seat across from him and the guard instructed her how to use the phones.

"Just pick it up and start talking. You could try without, but you'll hear better with the phone."

"Thank you."

"I'll be right outside the door. Holler if you need anything." The guard walked off and Jane lifted the handle of the phone, willing her hand to stop shaking as she did so. Drummond already had his phone glued to his ear.

"Thanks for coming," he said as a greeting.

"You're welcome." She waited for him to get to the point of this summons.

"Lovely weather we're having," he drawled. Jane said nothing.

"Okay, I can see you're not in the mood for polite chit-chat."

"Why am I here?" she asked.

"That is a very good question."

There was a long, increasingly uncomfortable silence as he simply looked her over and then smiled again. Jane felt her stomach flip over. The man was just vile.

Finally, he spoke again. "I need your help."

"You need my help? You do realize I'm no longer with the law firm? I'm out of the business entirely."

"Yes, I had heard that. Shame, really. You were an ace investigator."

"Well, almost getting killed has a way of making you reassess things. I decided I'd like to stay around a bit longer. Investigating no longer suits me."

Drummond made a face. "Getting up at the crack of dawn and making muffins and serving coffee suits you better? You can't be serious."

"I like it well enough." It unnerved her that he was so familiar with what she was doing now. How did he know that? She wouldn't put it past him to have someone find out where she was and what she was doing. No wonder she'd had nightmares lately.

"Hmmm. Well, I'm not sure I believe that. But, I'll let it go for now. I still think you can help me."

"Why would I want to help you? You're the one who tried to have me killed."

Drummond laughed. "Oh, that. Water under the bridge. Nothing personal, you understand. A simple misunderstanding."

"How do I know you won't try it again?" She narrowed her eyes at him.

"Like I said, I need your help. I have no reason to kill you." He smiled then and added, "Unless you give me one."

"Are you threatening me?" She stood up to leave. Coming here was a dumb idea. She should have known better.

"Please, wait. I'll be on my best behavior. Just hear me out," he implored and for the first time, she picked up something else in his voice—desperation. That made her curious. She sat back down and waited.

"So, here's the thing. I need a new lawyer. I really am innocent. Of what they are accusing me of, anyway. And I need a new legal team for my appeal. I want Nick himself to take it on."

Of all the things she could have imagined, this scenario had never crossed her mind. It didn't make any sense.

"You just met with Nick the other day. If you want his firm to represent you, why didn't you just ask him?"

"That seems so simple, doesn't it? But things are never as simple as they appear. His firm defended against me. They might not be inclined to switch sides now. But it's not only that."

He paused for a moment while Jane considered what he'd said. He was right, especially because Nick wasn't likely to want to take on a dog of a case. This one could make him look bad, as it didn't seem like there was any chance of the verdict being over-turned. Not based on what Jane knew, anyway.

"The thing is, I don't just want Nick's firm. I want you, too."

"He wants us to represent him? And you, too, as lead investigator? What did you tell him?" Nick buckled his seatbelt as he waited for Jane's response. They were sitting in his car, in the parking lot. Jane hadn't wanted to say much until they were well out of ear shot.

"I told him it was out of the question, for me, anyway. But that I'd talk to you and you can follow up. He didn't like that much, but he seemed to accept it. And he wished me well with my baking. It was disturbing to me that he knew so much about my life now. The whole exchange was odd. He's a strange one."

Nick was quiet and then said, "Well, I'm not inclined to accept, based on what we know. The case against him, though mostly circumstantial, seemed solid enough. Did he give you any information on why he thinks he has a chance?"

"No. He said you should think about it and then set up a meeting to discuss strategy. He seemed quite confident."

"The insane usually do," Nick chuckled.

"I don't think he's crazy. If anything, he's crazy like a fox. Cunning and manipulative, too. He is used to getting what he wants."

"Well, I'll talk to him. But, I still doubt we'll take it on. Wouldn't look good to take on a case this high profile unless we have a good shot at a reversal."

"I mentioned that to him. He just smiled."

Nick started the car and turned on the radio. They chatted comfortably during the drive back to Boston. It was the middle of the day, so traffic was light and about forty-five minutes later, Nick pulled into the parking garage off Boylston Street. As Jane opened her door and was about to get out and walk to her own, which was parked a few spots down, Nick spoke, "Thank you for doing this. Do you want me to keep you posted?"

For a brief second, Jane considered saying no, but then she smiled and said, "Sure, why not?"

13

Jane called Gramps on the way back to Waverly and invited him to come over for dinner that night. She told him that she'd fill him in on everything then. When she got closer to home, she stopped at the local Stop and Shop and picked up a package of her grandfather's favorite hot dogs and a box of macaroni and cheese. It was his favorite combination and every now and again, Jane liked a good hot dog, too.

When she got home, she fed Misty and then started making dinner. She set the hot dogs on a griddle to grill up when Gramps arrived, as they'd only take a few minutes. The mac and cheese was the orange powdered stuff, but Jane kicked it up a notch by stirring in a little extra butter and a splash of cream. Once it was all mixed, she poured it into a casserole dish and sprinkled a little parmesan cheese and panko crumbs on top along with a few more dots of butter and set it in the oven to lightly brown the top.

This was her compromise with her grandfather. If it was up to her, she'd make ooey-gooey macaroni and cheese from scratch, and Gramps would eat that, but she knew he preferred the boxed stuff. So, she made it her way. The crunchy bits on top were non-negotiable for her, and he admitted he liked them, too.

While she waited for Gramps to arrive, she poured herself a tiny glass of white wine and walked around the condo, checking to make sure that all the doors were securely locked and that the long piece of wood was in the bottom of the slider, to prevent it from opening if someone broke the lock. They would have to break the glass to get in.

Jane felt safe in her condo, as there were people on both sides of her and Gramps was just a few doors down. But the visit with Drummond had made her uneasy. He hadn't said as much, but it wouldn't surprise her if he'd had someone checking up on her.

He'd done that before when she was investigating him and he seemed familiar with her daily routine of the shop, though she supposed he could have just surmised that from newspaper coverage of Samantha Sellers' murder. She hoped that Nick would decide not to take his case, then she could forget all about Alex Drummond. That was the most likely outcome, based on what Nick had said earlier.

A few minutes later, there was a knock on the door and Gramps walked in holding a small bouquet of wild flowers.

"Thank you, those are beautiful!"

She took them from him and went searching for a vase to put them in. The flowers looked familiar, somehow.

"Gramps, where did you get these?"

"I picked them on the way over here," he said with a mischievous smile.

Jane chuckled. "Well, I hope no one saw you. I think it might be against the condo rules to pick the flowers from the landscaping."

"Oh, there's plenty more where those came from. They won't be missed."

Jane smiled as she slid the flowers into the vase and added water. "Thank you. They really are lovely. Have a seat. Dinner will be ready in a few minutes."

She turned the griddle on to cook the hotdogs and while it was heating up, she made her grandfather a Kahlua sombrero, his favorite cocktail. She knew he liked it with as little of the alcohol as possible, just enough to flavor the cream. She shook it up with the ice until it was nice and foamy, and then poured it in a glass and slid it across the counter. He was sitting in one of the stools at her kitchen island, watching her cook.

"So, fill me in. What did that rascal want?" he asked.

Jane told him about her meeting with Drummond and he was quiet for a moment when she finished. Then he took a long sip of his drink and mulled it over a bit more.

"I don't trust the guy. Maybe, just maybe, there's a slim chance that he didn't do the exact crime he was accused of, but I'd bet good money he did something that deserves jail time."

"I would totally agree with you on that." Jane took the casserole out of the oven and plated up their dinners, and then served Gramps and settled on the chair next to him. They were both quiet as they started to eat.

"This is outstanding, Janie. You're a good cook!" Jane smiled. Gramps was so easy. Everything was 'outstanding' to him.

He looked thoughtful, though, as he polished off the last of his hot dog.

"You don't suppose Nick will take him on as a client?"

"It's possible, but doubtful. He'll only take him on if he thinks he has a good chance of winning. He didn't seem to think that was the case, though."

"Maybe he doesn't know everything yet." Gramps said.

"Drummond did hint at that. I think he's full of it, though."

"Maybe so. None of your concern, though. We need to focus on this Samantha Sellers business."

Jane sighed. "I haven't the slightest idea who did this, and it sounds like Jake doesn't, either."

"He promised to get to the bottom of it," Gramps reminded her. "But he could use our help. I think we should try and talk to Maxine tomorrow."

"Samantha's friend?" Jane was surprised.

"She just bought a fancy new car, a gold Mercedes. Doesn't seem to be very sad about Samantha's death. She was driving around town yesterday with the top down."

That was interesting. "She bought a Mercedes convertible? I didn't realize the real estate market had picked up that much."

"Neither did I." Gramps reached for another hotdog. Jane smiled to herself. She was glad she'd cooked a few extras. Gramps liked to say he had the appetite of a bird, but he always went back for seconds, and sometimes thirds. As he happily munched, she thought about her schedule the following day.

"I can probably duck out of the shop mid-afternoon, after the lunch rush."

"I'll swing by to get you around two, then," Gramps confirmed.

Jane wondered how Maxine was able to afford such a nice car. She was fairly new to real estate. Her husband had divorced her just a few years before, and rumor was the only reason she got her real estate license and went to work was because she really needed the money.

"That sounds like a good plan. Now did you save room for dessert?" Jane cleared their plates and then pulled a carton of French vanilla ice cream out of the freezer. She knew Gramps would want to have a sundae with her. She'd inherited her sweet tooth from him.

"There's always room for dessert," he said with a smile.

A little after eight, Jane walked Gramps out and watched him stroll a few doors down to his unit. Her door was still open behind her and her body was tense, all her senses on alert. She was probably being a nervous Nellie, but she couldn't shake the worry that someone might be out there, watching.

Once Gramps was inside, she stepped back into her condo and locked the door tightly behind her and then engaged the deadlock. Once again, she checked every door and window, to make sure they were securely shut and locked, before pouring herself a glass of water and heading upstairs, Misty padding along behind her.

It was early, but she was ready to curl up in bed with a book. Misty jumped up on her bed and once she was settled, Jane did something she hadn't done in months. She got up and closed her bedroom door and locked it behind her. Then, she finally felt herself start to relax.

14

Jane woke to an impatient cat walking around on the pillow behind her head, stopping every minute or so to touch a soft paw to her cheek. After a few more taps, Jane felt a bit of claw. Misty was tired of being ignored. Meanwhile, the alarm on Jane's cell phone was ringing loudly. She'd managed to hit the snooze alarm twice and now, regretfully, it was time to get up and go make the donuts.

She dragged herself out of bed, fed Misty and then jumped in the shower to get ready for work. Thirty minutes later, she was on her way. She felt exhausted. She'd tossed and turned all night and got very little quality sleep. Unless she got a second wind, it was going to be a very long day.

The shop was quiet when she pulled into the back parking lot and then let herself into the kitchen. She turned on the radio, made a small pot of coffee for herself and then started to make the dough for donuts, and while that was rising, she began mixing the batter for the muffins.

An hour later, with the first batch of muffins baked and donuts ready to go into the fryer, she began to feel semi-human again. A half-pot of coffee definitely had helped.

Melissa walked in as she was pouring her third cup of rich black coffee. Melissa said hello, poured herself a cup of coffee and then got to work immediately, making pie crust. Today was chicken pot pie day.

"I think we may want to make double the amount we had last week," Melissa suggested. "Those pies are getting popular."

Jane had just been about to suggest that. Instead, she said, "That's a great idea."

They worked together, chatting every now and again. Just as Jane was getting ready to unlock the front door and let in their first customers, Melissa said, "Oh, I heard something about Jake that you might find interesting."

"Oh? What's that?" Jane stopped mid-step and turned her full attention to Melissa.

"I was in line behind him at the grocery store last night and overheard him talking on his cell phone. Said he wants to talk to you and might stop in this morning." Melissa smiled and added, "He also said he heard a rumor that your muffins are good."

Jane chuckled. "They are good! He probably heard that from Gramps." She was quiet for a moment and realized that Jake probably just wanted to ask her some follow-up questions. He didn't really want to just talk to her. Though that might be nice.

"He probably has more questions about the Samantha Sellers case," she said.

"Maybe. Or maybe he just wants an excuse to talk to you."

Jane raised her eyebrows. "I highly doubt that."

Melissa said nothing, just turned around and went back to rolling out pie dough.

"I'll be back to get you at two," Gramps said as he and his buddies headed toward the door. As usual, they'd been among her first customers. Jane went out back to grab some more blueberry muffins and after she finished re-stocking the muffin tray, she sensed that someone was at the register and stood up. She'd been crouching down as the blueberry muffins were on the bottom shelf. Jake was standing there.

"Hi, Jane. I decided it was time to try one of those blueberry muffins."

"Oh, good. This batch just came out of the oven." She popped one in a small paper bag and put it on the counter. "Anything else?"

"Sure, better add a medium black coffee. It's a two coffee kind of day."

Jane smiled at that. It was, indeed. She rang up his coffee and muffin, and then gave him his change. She expected Jake to immediately be on his way, but instead he lingered. There was no one behind him, so he didn't rush. Finally, he spoke.

"We're still not having much luck. I don't suppose you've heard anything from anyone?"

"Not yet, but Gramps and I are going to talk to Maxine at two."

"Maxine? Really?"

"Have you already talked to her?" she asked.

"Briefly. She didn't strike me as being particularly relevant."

"I wouldn't have thought so, either. It was Gramps idea, actually. He said she's been driving around town in a new Mercedes convertible."

"No kidding? I haven't seen that."

"He seemed surprised that she would have that kind of money."

"I wouldn't have expected it, either." Jake hesitated and then spoke quickly, "It's trivia tonight at the pub and buy-one-get-one pizza. Want to meet me there after work? We can share a bite to eat and you can tell me what you learned from Maxine."

Jane hesitated. What he was proposing sounded suspiciously like a date. She must have been silent a moment too long, because he quickly added, "It's no big deal. I just thought since we both have to eat, it might be good to compare notes and have some dinner. Maybe play a little trivia?" He smiled then and she noticed a dimple appear on one of his cheeks.

"I do like trivia. And pizza," she admitted. "What time should I meet you there?"

"Six is good. I'll get us a table."

Jake left and Jane found herself in a great mood the rest of the day. Even Gramps noticed when he stopped by at two to pick her up.

"Are you ready to go?"

"I'm ready!" Jane pulled off her apron and set in on the kitchen counter, then grabbed her purse and told Melissa she'd be back in about a half-hour.

"You seem a lot perkier than you did this morning," Gramps commented. "You kind of looked like something the cat dragged in, though of course you're still beautiful to me."

"Thanks. I didn't sleep great last night, but I seem to have found a second wind. I'll drive."

"So, what's our strategy?" Gramps asked as Jane pulled into the parking lot at Marksman's Realty where Maxine worked.

"I've been thinking about that. We can't just walk in and start asking her questions. I thought maybe we could ask her about that new retirement community that's opening soon."

"You mean where the old people live?" Gramps scoffed. Even at his age, he still considered himself too young to hang out with people in places like that. Jane had suggested more than once that he visit the senior center in town after her grandmother died, but he wanted no part of it.

"It's a fifty-five and over development. Hardly old," Jane said. "Besides, I know you don't ever want to go there, but we can just say we're gathering information. In case you ever decide to explore it."

"I won't." Gramps was firm about that.

"I hope you won't, either. But, it does give us a reason to talk to her."

"I suppose. Feels a bit dishonest, though."

"Well, truthfully we are just gathering information." Jane smiled. "Just in case you change your mind. And you can charm her at the same time. Tell her how much you admire her new car, get her to open up."

"Now I can see how you were so effective at investigating. You're creative and resourceful," Gramps said with admiration.

"Thank you. Hopefully, we'll learn something." Jane parked and they walked into the main reception area. There were several people on the phones, and one woman in her mid-forties with long, strawberry blonde hair, big, gold earrings and sunglasses that pushed her hair back got up when she saw them and walked over.

"Hi, I'm Maxine. Are you looking to buy a house?"

Gramps smiled and introduced the two of them and then added, "I'm not quite ready to buy yet, but if you have a minute, we wanted to get some information on that new development going in by the golf course."

"Riverhaven? The fifty-five plus community?"

"Yes, that's the one," Gramps confirmed.

"Well, come right this way. We can sit down and go over some information." Maxine led them to her office, which was a glassed-in room with two chairs facing her desk. They both sat and then Maxine led them through a series of basic questions about where Gramps was living now, what size unit he'd be interested in and, of course, his budget.

"I'm open on that. I have some flexibility if I do decide to move as long as it's the right place."

Maxine's eyes lit up at that and Jane felt a pang of guilt. She didn't want to keep her too long from other potentially real clients. She gave Gramps a little nudge with her shoe, and caught his eye and silently signaled him to get to the point and wrap it up.

"So, Maxine, I saw you zipping around town the other day. That's quite the car you have. I must say I'm tempted to get a convertible myself." Gramps was laying it on thick and Maxine ate it up.

"Isn't it great? I love it. That was a well-deserved present to myself."

"That's quite a present," Jane said in an awestruck tone full of reverence.

Maxine smiled. "I know. Though there's a little sadness attached. I was a beneficiary on Samantha's life insurance policy. She'd told me once she was changing that when she was going through the divorce, but I never really thought much of it—until I got a call from her lawyer. It's just awful, what happened to Samantha, truly terrible. But for me, it was like a Christmas bonus, unexpected and very much appreciated."

"Wow, that's amazing," Gramps said.

"Odd that her husband wasn't the beneficiary," Jane said.

"Yes, ordinarily he would have been. Maxine changed that as soon as she started the divorce proceedings. It was an individual policy that she paid for herself."

"You must have been very close to her. I am sorry for your loss." Gramps said.

Maxine frowned. "We used to be close, years ago. Not so much in recent years. Like I said, I was surprised to get that call. I really didn't think she meant it when she said she was going to change it."

"Was it a while ago that she made the change? Maybe that's why you didn't think of it."

"Not that long ago—six months, maybe? She was kind of joking around, said she owed me." Maxine's face clouded over then and she glanced at the clock on the wall.

"I'm sorry, I just realized the time. I'm afraid I have to run to a showing. Let me know when you are ready to take a look at one of the model units at Riverhaven. I'd be happy to show it to you. In the meantime, here's a brochure with all the details." She handed Gramps a colorful brochure and stood up, which was their signal to go.

"I'll do that. Thank you." Gramps shook her hand, and then he and Jane headed off to the car.

"What did you make of that?" Jane asked as they buckled up and she started the engine.

"Well, it's clear they had a bumpy relationship. She did seem surprised, though. Unless she's a good actress, I don't think she's involved."

Jane wasn't so sure. "It seemed to me like she realized she said too much and regretted it."

"Maybe so. Maybe Jake can dig a little deeper," Gramps suggested.

"I'll let him know. I'm seeing him tonight after work."

"Oh, really? That's interesting." Gramps had a twinkle in his eye.

"It's nothing like that," Jane protested.

"Okay. Well, keep me posted."

"I will."

15

The pub was crowded when Jane arrived a few minutes past six. Normally, a Tuesday night wouldn't be overly busy anywhere in town, but the pub's buy-one-get-one pizza deal brought people out in droves. It was really good pizza. Jane made her way through the bar traffic to the restaurant section just beyond and saw Jake already seated at a booth.

"You made it. I forgot how busy it gets here. It's been a while since I've been in on a Tuesday," Jake said as she sat across from him.

"Gramps comes in a lot. He and David like their pizza." Jane's cousin David had a standing date with their grandfather, and they often came on Thursdays when the pizza deal was offered early in the evening, from four to six, as Thursday nights later on were plenty busy enough.

"We can each order whatever we like and share. Does that work for you?" Jake suggested.

"Perfect." The waitress came by then and they both ordered draft IPAs from a local brewery and their pizza. Jane went with a margarita, which was pesto, mozzarella and fresh tomato and Jake got a meat lover's special with sausage, hamburger, sausage and onion.

"That sounds good, too," she said after they'd put their order in.

"Yours does, too, but I need a little meat on mine." Jake grinned and Jane felt a flutter in her stomach. It might not be one, but it did sort of feel like a date and Jane was surprised to find she liked the feeling—though she quickly reminded herself that it was likely all in her mind. Jake was a professional and wouldn't consider dating someone who was part of an active investigation. She was snapped out of her mini-daydream by him asking about their meeting with Maxine.

"Did you learn anything interesting?" he asked as the waitress set down their beers.

"I'm not sure if there's any connection, but Maxine did say that the money for the Mercedes came from Samantha Sellers' life insurance policy."

"Maxine was her beneficiary? That seems odd."

"I agree. She said she changed it about six months ago as they were going through the terms of their divorce."

"They must have been really close."

"She said they were once, but it didn't sound like that was the case anymore. She admitted that she was surprised by the call from the attorney. She hadn't thought Samantha was serious about putting it in her name. She mentioned something about Samantha owing her, but I think she realized she'd said too much. She clammed up right after that."

"That is highly unusual, to change the beneficiary like

that. Even in divorce, it often stays with the ex-spouse, at least for a period of time, until everything else is settled." Jake looked thoughtful and was quiet for a moment.

"Is Maxine in a relationship with anyone?" Jane wondered.

"I don't know. You didn't ask?" He sounded surprised and Jane immediately felt annoyed.

"How, exactly, would I have casually asked that?"

"I guess that would have been somewhat awkward," he agreed.

Dan, the trivia leader, stopped by their table then to see if they planned to stay and play trivia, which would be starting momentarily.

Jake looked at her before answering him. "What do you think?"

"Sure, why not?" Dan was happy with that response and dropped off a score sheet and notepad for their answers. Jane had always enjoyed playing team trivia and felt a moment of sadness as she remembered playing often after work in Boston with some of her colleagues from the office.

She and Jake did well on the first few questions, which were in categories each of them liked—food for Jane and history for Jake. Soon after, the waitress brought their pizzas and they dove in.

An hour-and-a-half later, full of pizza and happy with their second place finish and ten-dollar gift card they could use on a future visit, they got ready to leave. The waitress had just dropped off their check and Jane immediately reached for her wallet, intending to split the bill evenly with Jake. But he wouldn't hear of it.

"I invited you here. Dinner's on me."

"You don't have to do that. It's not like this is a date," she protested.

Jake was quiet for a moment and then said, "It's really like I'm just buying you a few beers, since one of the pizzas was free. It's not a big deal. I'm glad you were able to join me."

He made it sound so sensible. "Okay. Thank you, then."

"You're welcome. But we have to do it again soon. We have that gift card to use and we need a first place finish next time."

Jane laughed. "Okay, but next time it's on me."

"We can discuss that later." Jake stood, and as Jane slid out of the booth she did a double-take and tapped Jake's arm.

"That might answer the question about Maxine's relationship." Maxine was sitting at the bar and leaning over to kiss her on the cheek before settling into the chair next to her was Chester Sellers.

"Hmmm, interesting. Maybe it's not what it looks like," Jake said.

"Right. Maybe they're just good friends. Do you really believe that?" Jane asked.

"Not especially. But you never know. They might just be affectionate with each other."

Jane said nothing and Jake added, "It's worth looking into."

16

Jake went into work a little earlier than usual the next morning. He had the feeling that they were missing something on the Samantha Sellers' case. On the surface, it seemed simple enough. Someone wanted Samantha Sellers dead—most likely someone she knew.

They'd spoken to everyone they could think of who had any connection to her. But since they didn't have any solid suspects yet, they hadn't been able to request a copy of the will. Now that he was aware of Maxine's bequest, he could officially speak with her again and put that request in. It would be interesting to see if the will held any other surprises. And, of course, one of the first questions he asked of everyone he spoke with was, "Do you benefit in any way by the death of Samantha Sellers?" Everyone he had spoken to had said no, but he probably talked to them all before the will was read.

He was still scratching his head about the connection to Jane Cho. He didn't think for even a minute that Jane was involved. He was professional enough to detach himself from his opinion and still investigate thoroughly, but logically it didn't add up. Jane was simply too smart to leave a body on her own premises with a note that seemed to suggest a connection. Especially given her background.

If Jane had been involved, he doubted there even would have been a body to find. With her investigative experience, she'd be far more careful. And it didn't make sense. So Samantha had filed a lawsuit to shut her down? There were no real grounds for that, so Jane had nothing to worry about. Samantha was just a nuisance, but not one worth killing for. But someone must have benefited by Samantha being gone, and he would get to the bottom of it.

He thought back to the night before at the restaurant, when he and Jane had seen both Maxine and Chester at the bar. It was surprising how they seemed to be so friendly. Were they just good friends, since Maxine had been Samantha's best friend? Given the animosity between Samantha and her soon to be ex-husband, though, it did seem odd that Maxine would be so chummy with him. Loyal friends didn't typically behave like that.

Jake didn't like it when there were so many loose ends. He needed to get his report together to share with the state police who would soon be taking the case over. In Massachusetts, only the larger cities like Boston, and Worcester and a few others had their own homicide investigative units. The other, smaller towns handled the initial investigation and then handed their findings over to the state police.

That was one thing that had been difficult for Jake to get used to, since he came to Waverly from the Boston precinct and had been a homicide detective. He left that work for a reason, but still, old habits died hard and although Jake would still work with the state police in assisting as much as possible, he was hoping to hand them more complete findings to run with.

He was just finishing up a summary of the case so far, when there was a knock on his office door. Usually, he left his door open, but he'd closed it so he could focus without interruption and cross this report of his to-do list. He heard the door open and smiled as he turned around. Only one person would walk in without waiting for an invitation.

"Hi, Mom." His mother, Marcia Tolino, all five feet of her, stood in the middle of his office, holding a plastic container out to him.

"What's that?" he asked her.

"You were too busy to come by last night, so I brought the meatballs to you. I can't eat them all myself, you know."

His mouth watered at the thought of his mother's meatballs and sauce. He'd forgotten to pack a lunch.

"Thank you. But you didn't have to do that."

"There's stuffed shells, too. Your favorite. Have you lost weight?"

"No, Mom. I'm pretty sure I'm the same as always."

"You look thinner to me. Can't have you fade away to nothing. You need to keep your strength up," his mother fussed as she set his lunch on the corner of his desk.

"I'm sorry I wasn't able to stop by last night. I had plans."

"Yes, you told me. How was your date?" She had seated herself in the chair directly across from Jake's desk, and leaned forward, eager for his response.

"Mom, I told you it wasn't a date."

"That's what you said. But you met her at a restaurant, shared a meal and played that silly game you like. Sounds like a date to me."

"It wasn't. I promise you that."

"Are you going out again?"

Were they? Jake hoped so.

"I don't know. Maybe."

"I see. But, it's not a date."

Jake sighed. "No, Mom. Jane is just a friend."

His mother shook her head at that and then stood.

"I'll leave you to your work. I have to get to the gym, anyway. Water aerobics is in forty-five minutes."

Jake smiled at that. His mother was a ball of energy. She couldn't sit still for long. She was a wonderful cook and a great mother, and ever since his father died five years ago, she'd turned the fussing up a notch. She was dying to be a grandmother, and to see him settled. Thankfully, though, his brother, Jeremy, had taken the pressure off a bit by having twins a year ago.

"Bye, Mom. Have fun. Thanks for the meatballs."

When she left, his thoughts turned back to Jane Cho. Truth be told, he wouldn't mind going on a real date with her. But that would have to wait.

17

What? You took his case? Are you serious? Hold on a sec." Jane turned to Melissa, who was bringing a new tray of muffins to the front. "Melis, can you watch the register for a minute? I'll be right back. Mrs. Cosby had her usual blueberry and medium coffee, black."

"Sure thing."

Melissa set down the muffins and jumped in to help while Jane walked out back to give Nick her full attention.

"Okay, sorry about that. So, fill me in." Jane was shocked that Nick had decided to represent Alex Drummond. She didn't think there was a realistic chance that would happen.

"I know. I surprised myself on this one. But, I went to meet with him yesterday and as you know, he can be persuasive. It's a compelling case and an intriguing challenge. I haven't had a case I could really sink my teeth into for a while. This could be it."

"I thought you generally avoided this kind of case. Didn't you say it seemed like a dog?" Jane reminded him.

"Well, yeah. That's what I thought at first. But Alex and I got to talking and I have to tell you. I really don't think he did it."

Jane found a chair and sat down. She'd always thought Nick was one of the smartest lawyers she'd ever worked with. Had he fallen under Drummond's spell? Was his judgment clouded?

"Is there any new information? His case was mostly circumstantial, but the jury did find him guilty. He had plenty of motive for each of the killings."

"Well, that's the thing. It turns out that he's not the only one with a real motive."

"He gave you something on someone else? Why didn't he share this before?"

"I don't think he ever thought he would need to. He was pretty confident that he'd get off. All the evidence was purely circumstantial, and he had a good legal team."

"Not good enough," Jane said. "And he didn't count on you being so good. Getting that employee he framed off only made him look that much guiltier."

"True," Nick admitted. "But we don't actually know if Nick framed the kid. What if someone else did?"

"Like who?" In spite of herself, Jane was fascinated by the shift in direction that Nick was exploring.

"Well, I can tell it pains him to consider it. It seemed hard for him to tell me this, but it sounds like he suspects that his stepson may be involved."

"Which one?" Jane asked. Alex had twin stepsons. One

worked in the family software business. The other had followed a different path and was on the leadership track within South Boston's Irish mafia.

"That's the problem. He's not sure which one. Both of them have a potential motive. They are equal shareholders in Drummond's software empire," Nick said.

"And even given the publicity, Drummond's stock is up," Jane said in disgust.

"Hard for it not to be," Nick agreed. "With the chief architects at his two main competitors gone, it slowed their releases and let Drummond's take control of the market."

Both of the men who were killed were instrumental in new product development at their respective companies. The initial PR had been damaging, but the stock quickly rebounded when Drummond's innovative new release hit the market and took off.

"He must have some idea which one might have been involved?"

"He said he keeps going back and forth on that. Says he could see either of them being involved. I don't think there's any love lost there."

"So he needs you to figure that out, too? Which one is the most likely suspect?" Jane asked.

"Nice, huh? Are you temped? It's a dream case. Unlimited billing. Whatever it takes to get it done. He said we have an open checkbook, so to speak." Nick sounded excited and much to her dismay, Jane felt a hint of the old excitement she used to feel whenever she started a new case, too. She was tempted. He knew she would be.

"Not tempted in the least," she lied.

Nick was silent for a moment and then in a cheerful voice said, "That's too bad. Well, if you change your mind let me know."

"I will." And then Jane couldn't help asking, "Who are you putting on it?"

"To investigate? Liza I think."

"Liza. That's good." Liza Kennedy had been with the firm as long as Nick had. She was a good, reliable investigator. She was slow and steady and for a client with unlimited pockets, it was a perfect match. Jane sighed. It was just as well. Guilty or not, Alex Drummond was the last person she'd want to help, anyway.

"I should get back to work," she said and started walking toward the register.

"Right. Same here. I'll talk to you soon, Jane."

Jane hung up the phone and thought about what Nick had just said. Even if it turned out that one of his stepsons was the actual killer, she still found it difficult to believe that Alex Drummond wasn't involved in any of those deaths. But, it wasn't her problem to worry about any longer. No, her biggest decision for the rest of the day would be whether or not to make another batch of blueberry muffins.

She'd just decided to make them when the front door chimed and a new customer walked in. Jane was surprised to see that it was Ellen Smith. She usually came first thing in the morning, on her way to the high school.

"Hi, Ellen. School get out early today?" she teased. The other woman smiled.

"Yes, actually. It's a half-day, so I decided to treat myself to an iced cappuccino."

"That's great. Coming right up." The shop was almost completely empty except for one table in the corner. Jane handed her the cold drink, took her money and then said, "Do you have a moment to chat?"

18

ure, I have a few minutes," Ellen agreed.

"Great, let's sit for a minute." Jane led her to a small table in the corner. Aside from two regulars who were working away on their laptops, the shop was empty. Jane knew that Melissa could handle any stray customers that might wander in. She settled into a seat and waited for Ellen to join her.

As soon as she did, Jane spoke. "I was having dinner with my sister-in-law the other night and she mentioned that you were good friends with Samantha Sellers. Since she was discovered here on the property, I've been wondering what happened to her."

Ellen took a sip of her drink and looked sad.

"She was a good friend. It's so upsetting—and to think something like that could happen here. I've always felt so safe in Waverly."

"Me, too," Jane agreed. "I still do, for the most part." She paused for a moment and then carefully said, "They say that something like ninety-five percent of all murders are done by someone who knew the victim. In a way, that makes me feel safer."

"I suppose," Ellen agreed. "Though I can't imagine who could do this to Sam."

"There's no one in her life that you were aware of that she had conflict with?"

"No," Ellen said immediately and then added, "The only person she had any issues with that I knew of was Chester and he's harmless. It was just your usual divorce tensions."

Jane shared her opinion on Chester. She didn't think he was the one who did this.

"Was there anything else going on in her life that was stressful that you were aware of?"

Ellen took a sip of her coffee and looked deep in thought, as if she was debating saying something. Twice, she opened her mouth to speak and then took another sip of her drink instead.

"What is it?" Jane finally asked.

Ellen sighed. "Well, I don't know if it's important or relevant at all, which is why I didn't mention anything before when that cop came to talk to me, but Samantha was under quite a bit of financial stress."

Jane was surprised. "She was? I thought the bed and breakfast was doing well?"

"It's holding its own, but that's not the issue." Ellen leaned forward and looked around the room first, to make sure that no one was listening. "Samantha had a little bit of a gambling problem. She'd lost quite a lot of money recently. She even asked to borrow money from me."

"Really? What did she need the money for? To gamble?"

"She said it was to pay back the people she owed money to. They let her run up an account and she went into the red."

That was interesting.

"Where did she gamble?" Jane assumed she was talking about Foxwoods or Mohegan Sun, the two closest casinos, both of which were several hours away, in Connecticut.

"No, she didn't bother with those places anymore. She went to the underground clubs in Mumford."

"She did?" Jane was surprised and intrigued by that. She'd heard rumors of these underground casinos but wasn't sure they really existed. Supposedly, they were pop-up gambling operations. Each weekend, they were in a different location and only those on their special VIP list were notified with the current addresses.

"Yes, she started going a few months ago. Someone invited her and she won a little bit of money, and then she was hooked. She started going almost every weekend, except that after that first weekend or two she hardly ever won."

"Where were these pop-up places?"

"She said it varied. Sometimes a private hall, other times a business or someone's home."

"That sounds risky," Jane said. It was clever too, though, and she could understand the need to rotate the location.

"I thought so, too, but she said it was all very organized and super-secret. They are very careful who they allow in."

"Did she get into trouble with these people?" Jane asked.

Ellen bit her lower lip and then said, "She said that she owed a lot of money and they'd been calling and harassing her. She wasn't allowed to come to the clubs anymore. They were showing up at her house at all hours, demanding their money."

Jane didn't like the sound of that. "That must have been very stressful for her."

"She said it was terrifying, actually," Ellen said with a shudder. She held on to her coffee cup with both hands, as if she needed its warmth.

"When did she tell you this?"

"She first mentioned it a little over a month ago, and then again just last week. Some guy had stopped by her house again and she was a bit shaken up."

"Did she ever mention any of their names?"

"Only their first names. The main guy that was harassing her had an unusual name. At first, I thought she said Lenny, but it was actually Lanny. I don't know what that's short for though."

"Lanny. Okay, that's a start anyway. If you think of anything else, please let me know."

"I will." As Ellen stood up, her eyes watered. "I really miss her. I hope they catch whoever did this."

"So do I."

19

W e could go check out that Mumford casino if you
want," Gramps suggested. They were sitting on Jane's
back patio, enjoying bowls of the banana 'ice-cream' that Jane
often made for them. It was simply frozen bananas, a splash
of vanilla and a bit of raspberry jam, whizzed up in a food
processor until it turned into a gelato-like confection that was
surprisingly creamy and healthier than ice-cream—though
Gramps always insisted on having hot fudge, whipped cream
and sprinkles on his.

"I'd love to, but how do you supposed we do that? You
have to know someone to get in." Jane hadn't gambled in a
long time. She did enjoy a game of blackjack every now and
again, though. Because of her aptitude with math and computers, she'd learned years ago that it was surprisingly easy to
count cards, and it often gave her an edge.

"Maybe I know someone," Gramps said mysteriously.

"You do? Who?" Gramps never failed to surprise her.

"Carl likes to go every now and again. He's a monster at blackjack," he said proudly.

"Carl is? I never would have guessed. And I didn't know you'd ever been."

"It's something to do. I don't tell you everything, you know." Gramps winked at her. "I can get a little wild and crazy sometimes." He frowned then and asked, "Do we have any more whipped cream? It doesn't look like I took enough."

Jane smiled. "I'll get it for you."

She went into the kitchen, and then returned with the can of whipped cream and gave a good squirt to the rest of Gramps' dessert.

"That's better, thanks. You make good ice-cream, Janie."

"So, you think Carl can get us in?"

"He will if I ask him to. He'll have to come with us, though."

"That's fine. Do they do this every weekend?" she asked.

"Like clockwork. It's all done by email now. Goes out Friday morning."

"Email? Really? That doesn't seem very safe." Jane set her empty dish on the patio table, wishing she'd made a bigger batch.

"Oh, they're very careful. It's all in code. Like a party invitation. It mentions the street names as if they are people's names, so for that Moose Lodge on Mulberry Street. It might say something like, 'The Mulberry family invites you to join them at gathering on Friday.'"

"That is clever," Jane agreed. Then she couldn't help but ask, "Do you feel guilty at all going there? I mean, it is against the law."

Gramps shook his head. "It's harmless. Besides, I'm retired. Don't have to answer to anyone anymore."

"That's true," she agreed.

"I'll talk to Carl tomorrow at coffee. We'll make a plan for Friday."

Friday night around six, Gramps and Carl picked Jane up and they headed off to Mumford. It felt a bit surreal to Jane to be sitting in the backseat of Carl's mint green Cadillac as they drove to an illicit gambling hall. Both Gramps and Carl were enthusiastic about the outing. Carl was wearing a brightly colored Hawaiian print shirt that he said was his lucky charm.

"I wear this every time I go. Hasn't failed me yet."

Gramps looked equally festive in his best, baby-blue button-down golf shirt that flattered his abundance of snow white hair. Jane hadn't been at all sure how to dress, and had finally settled on a simple black skirt and scoop-necked black and white sleeveless top. Fairly conservative, except for her fun, candy-apple red, three-inch pumps. Gramps had shaken his head when he saw them.

"I don't know how you can even walk in those things?"

"Very carefully!" she had said and laughed. Jane loved a pretty pair of shoes and didn't get the opportunity to wear them much anymore. Around the shop, she mostly wore comfortable sneakers, so her feet wouldn't ache too much from standing on them all day. At night, she usually walked around barefoot. So, it was only on the rare occasion that she went out at night, that she got a chance to wear her favorite shoes.

"Where is it being held tonight?" Jane asked as they crossed the town line into Mumford. Mumford was twice the size of Waverly and had its fair share of questionable areas. Cute and quaint it was not.

"It's the Stephens' family party tonight," Carl said with a chuckle. "A karate studio on Stephens Street. There's a huge basement. I've been there before."

"A karate studio. Who would guess it?" Jane said.

"Exactly," Gramps agreed. "This is going to be fun, Janie. I brought plenty of dollar bills."

When they pulled into the parking lot at the Keane Karate building, there were only a few spots left, and the parking lot was huge. There were no other businesses around, so Jane guessed most of the cars must be here for the same reason they were.

Carl parked and then led the way. They followed him to the front door where a giant, muscular man with a crew-cut and angry, dark tattoos on both arms politely asked their names. Carl told him and then the bouncer checked his list. Once he was satisfied that they were on it, he opened the door and welcomed them in.

"I think you've been here before," he said to Carl. "Everyone is downstairs. Enjoy yourself, and good luck."

20

Jane walked carefully down the steep steps to the basement. The stairs were covered in an old, frayed green carpet that kept catching on the bottom of Jane's heels. She slowed a little and held tight to the railing as she followed Gramps and Carl. Once they reached the basement, it took her eyes a moment to adjust. It was dark down there. There were lights everywhere, but they were dim and it was smoky. Smoking wasn't allowed in any public buildings any longer, but Jane supposed that didn't apply to illegal clubs, and smoking did sort of fit the overall ambiance.

She was surprised at the size of the crowd. It was like a large party, probably around a hundred and fifty or so people. At least a half-dozen blackjack tables were set up in the middle of the room, and along the sides, an equal number of poker tables. One large roulette wheel was in the corner and on the opposite end of the room, two different groups were playing craps. They eyed the blackjack tables and Carl explained how it worked.

"Early in the night, there's no minimum amount you have to bet. They want everyone in and hooked as soon as they get here. Then once everyone has had a drink or two, they raise the stakes. Every hour, they increase the minimum bet. That's why we like to come early."

Gramps appeared to be half-listening. He was busy scouting the room to find a table with three empty seats. "Over here!"

He led them to a table where three college-aged young men had just left to go sit at the bar. There was a makeshift bar that spanned the length of the longest wall. Jane and Carl sat on either side of Gramps and placed their bets for the next round. They all put two dollars down. While the dealer dealt the hand, Jane looked around the room, trying to get a sense of who was running things. It was hard to tell at first, but there were two men standing at the end of the bar who seemed to be keeping an eye on everything, and neither of them was drinking.

Jane deliberately didn't pay attention to how the cards were dealt on this round. She wanted to appear somewhat clueless about the game, so that when she started to win it could seem like beginner's luck. She didn't want to draw attention to herself. Even if she had been counting cards, it probably wouldn't have helped in the first round anyway as her cards were terrible. She asked for another card when it was her turn and then was instantly out when her total went over twenty-one. Both Gramps and Carl won their hands.

Jane paid closer attention on the next few hands and deliberately lost one hand and won the next. Gramps and Carl won both hands, let their winnings ride and then lost it all on the last hand.

"Easy come, easy go," Carl said.

Gramps made a face. "So much more fun when we win, though." He glanced at Janie's stack of winning chips and smiled. "Like riding a bike for you, huh?"

Jane kicked him lightly under the table, a warning to keep his voice down.

"Beginner's luck!" she said brightly as the dealer gathered all the cards and started shuffling.

They played at that table for another hour. Every so often a pretty—usually blond—cocktail waitress came by to see if they would like a drink. Carl and Gramps never had more than one. Jane nursed the glass of white wine, as she needed to have her wits about her and when the time was right, she intended to order another drink at the bar.

By the end of the hour, both Carl and Gramps were very happy to be ahead about fifty dollars each. Jane had continued to bid carefully, yet in a way that made it look like she didn't really know what she was doing, deliberately losing several rounds and then doubling down randomly and winning. She had over five hundred dollars in front of her when she decided to take a break and head to the bar. She pushed her stack of chips toward Gramps and gave up her seat.

"Can you keep an eye on this for me? I'm going to take a break and head to the bar for a minute. Would either of you like anything?" she offered. They both declined and turned their attention back to the next round. The two men that she had spotted earlier were still standing by the bar, chatting and glancing around the room intently. She'd noticed that they'd glanced her way more than once. She smiled at them as she found a seat at the bar, a few feet away from where they stood. The bartender made his way over to her and she ordered another glass of wine, a surprisingly decent chardonnay.

She'd hoped to just sit close enough to them that she might overhear something useful. But within minutes of her drink arriving, one of the men slid into the seat next to her and struck up a conversation.

"I don't think I've seen you here before. Are you having a good time?" His words were polite, charming even, but as he spoke, he was also keeping an eye on the rest of the room. He looked vaguely familiar to her, but she couldn't place where she might have seen him before. He was tall, with longish, dark brown hair that he wore tucked behind his ears, giving him a shaggy, hip look. Wire-rimmed glasses completed the image.

"Yes, lots of fun. I'm here with my grandfather and his friend, Carl."

"Ah, Carl. Yes, we see him every now and again." He held out his hand. "I'm Landon."

"Jane," she replied as she shook his hand.

"I couldn't help but notice you had a nice run of luck just now. Do you play blackjack much?"

"Thank you. No, I haven't played in years, but it's such a fun game." That was true. It had been several years since she'd played. She smiled sweetly and added, "I do feel really lucky."

Landon considered her comment for a moment, and then smiled and said, "Well, we'd love to see more of you. Be sure to sign the guestbook on the way out, and we'll add you to the email invite list."

"Oh, could you? That would be great. I'd love to bring a friend sometime, if that's okay?"

"We have a rule that you have to come to three parties, either alone or with another vetted member, before you can bring a guest." Landon grinned and his face took on a boyish, mischievous look. "What we're doing here isn't exactly legal. So we have to be careful. I hope you understand."

"Of course. I look forward to coming back again soon."

Just then, the other man walked over and tapped Landon on the shoulder. He leaned in and spoke softly so Jane couldn't hear what he said, but whatever it was got Landon's attention. He stood immediately, and his eyes swept the room.

"If you'll excuse me? It was very nice to meet you, Jane."

And then he was gone, off to a far corner of the room to confer with several other men, older men who looked to be in their late-fifties or even early sixties. After a heated discussion, the men and Landon disappeared upstairs. Jane took her drink back to the blackjack table and rejoined Gramps and Carl. Their piles of chips looked about the same, meaning they were winning and losing.

"As long as I don't go too deep into the red, I could play this for hours," Gramps said with a smile.

Jane slid into the last empty chair and they played for another hour, until Carl lost two hands in a row and declared that it was a good time to wrap up.

"I feel like lady luck has left the building and maybe so should we," he said.

Gramps yawned. "Okay by me."

They gathered up their winnings and cashed their chips in before they left. Gramps was down by about twenty dollars, Carl was up by thirty and Jane was still holding about five hundred dollars. She'd been careful not to win too often and was happy with her take for the night.

As they approached downtown Waverly, it was about nine-thirty.

"Anyone feel like stopping for an ice-cream? Mitchell's Dairy is open until ten." Carl said as he turned on to Main Street.

"Always room for ice-cream. Janie?" Gramps asked.

"Sure."

They joined the long line outside, and once they had their ice creams, they settled at one of the empty picnic tables to eat them.

"So, what did you think, Janie?" Gramps asked.

"It was fun, and interesting."

"Did you learn anything?"

"Not really. I only chatted with one of the organizers for a few minutes before he got called away to what looked like some kind of emergency."

"You know who that was, right?" Carl asked.

"He looked somewhat familiar. Said his name was Landon. I didn't catch his last name. I don't think he mentioned it."

"That was Lanny. Lanny Drummond. He was in the news when his stepfather was indicted for murder."

"That was Lanny?" No wonder he looked familiar.

The sophisticated Landon was the Lanny that had been harassing Samantha.

"We need to go back next weekend." Alex Drummond's mobster son was one of the last people to see Samantha Sellers before she was murdered and Jane wanted another chance to talk to him.

"We can do better than that," Carl said. "There's a party tomorrow night. On Mulberry, this time."

"You sure you don't mind going again so soon? I don't want to disrupt your Saturday night," Jane said.

Both Gramps and Carl laughed at that.

"Don't be silly, honey. Now we have plans!"

21

Saturdays were always crazy busy at the shop. There was a non-stop flow of customers until almost two in the afternoon. Melissa took a break then, to grab a bite to eat, while Jane poured herself an iced coffee and snuck a bite of a blueberry muffin in between customers. She had just popped the last piece in her mouth when the front door chimed and Jake walked in.

"I need another one of your muffins," he said, smiling. "And a tall iced coffee." Jane got his order together and while she was ringing him up, he asked, "So, how are you?"

Jane smiled as she handed him his change. "I'm good! Keeping busy."

"Have you been up to anything I should know about?" he asked.

There was no one else in the shop now, so Jane took her time answering. "I've had a few interesting conversations.

Ellen was in the other day and mentioned that Samantha was having some financial issues brought on by a gambling addiction. She owed a lot of money to one of those under-ground casinos."

"Like the one that operates out of Mumford?" he asked

"You know about that?" Janie had wondered if the local police were aware of the illegal casinos.

"I've heard rumors every now and again."

"I went last night," Janie admitted.

Jake looked surprised. "You did? Who did you go with? I heard you have to know someone to be allowed in."

"I do know someone. One of Gramps' friends goes every now and then. He took us."

Jake chuckled at that. "That is funny that your grandfather condoned it."

"I teased him about that, too. He said it doesn't matter now that he's retired. He had a blast."

"Do you gamble?" Jake asked.

"I like to play a little blackjack every now and then. But it had been several years since I last played."

"How did you do?"

"I won a little money," Jane admitted. "But the most in-teresting thing was that I met the person that Ellen said had been harassing Samantha. Lanny Drummond. I didn't realize who it was, though, until after I'd already left. He introduced himself as Landon."

"You met the infamous Lanny? What was he like?"

Jane thought about that for a moment. "Not what you would expect. He was charming, actually, and seemed very smart. If I'd met him in another setting, I would have guessed he was a software entrepreneur, like his father possibly. Certainly not a blue collar thug."

"Right. Well, there's nothing blue collar about Lanny. Seems like he is following in his stepfather's footsteps as a sharp business person and entrepreneur, though on the opposite side of the law."

"I can't picture him harassing anyone, though. He seems too polished for that," Jane said.

"Maybe he delegates that part of the business?" Jake suggested.

That hadn't occurred to Jane. She would have to talk to Ellen again and find out more.

"You may be right about that."

A customer walked in then and Jane took his order at the register. Jake looked like he wanted to stay and talk a bit longer, but as soon as Jane finished making change, several more customers walked in.

"Jane, I'll catch up with you later." Jake left as Melissa returned from her lunch break and for the next few hours, they had a steady stream of customers. But by a quarter to four, the store emptied out and they ran around cleaning up before it was time to close.

As Jane was taking out the trash, her cell phone rang and it was Gramps.

"We still on for tonight?" He sounded excited and Jane smiled.

"Yes, see you at six again?"

"It's a date!"

Jane decided to take a different approach with her outfit this time. She blew her hair out and then used a curling iron to add loose curls that gave it a pretty, tousled look. She wore one of her favorite tops, a rose pink knit that was cut a hint lower than she normally wore. Jane didn't have any cleavage to speak of, but a push up bra worked wonders in boosting what curves she did have. A pair of snug, faded jeans and sexy, leather sandals with a flattering, high heel and her look was complete. She knew she'd pulled it off by Gramps and Carl's reactions.

"Wow, Janie, you look pretty!" Carl said.

"You clean up good, kid," Gramps said.

Carl drove again and the location this time was a private function hall on Mulberry Street. The set-up was similar, too, and this time, the bouncer recognized all of them.

"Nice to see you all again. Head on in," he said with a smile.

"They're friendly here," Jane commented as they stepped inside.

"It's because we have a pretty girl with us," Carl said as he led the way.

There weren't as many people as there had been the night before. Jane wondered out loud if it started later on Saturdays.

"Usually, it is a slower start," Carl confirmed. "It will get hopping later."

"We have our pick of the tables this time," Gramps said with enthusiasm as they surveyed the room.

"You decide," Jane said.

Gramps led them to the one blackjack table that was

completely empty. The dealer stood there, waiting for his first customers to arrive. They settled in and placed their first bets. There was no sign of Lanny—or Landon as Jane thought of him.

They played for over an hour before the room started to pick up and other people joined their table. To entertain herself, Jane focused intently on counting the cards and won five hands in a row. Then she noticed the dealer suddenly paying close attention to her and she stopped counting and deliberately lost several hands in a row. Out of the corner of her eye, she noticed Lanny stroll in and head for the bar. He chatted with the bartender for a moment, and then stood watching the room as he sipped what looked like a glass of water. Suddenly, Jane was thirsty.

"Looks like my luck is turning," she said with a laugh as both Gramps and Carl won their hands.

"You can't win them all, Janie-girl," Gramps said.

"I'm going to take a break and go get another glass of wine." Jane made her way to the bar, and settled into a chair and waited for the bartender to come over to her. Lanny caught her eye as soon as she sat down and she smiled back at him. He accepted the invitation and walked over. He didn't sit, though, but rather leaned against the chair next to her, still keeping his eyes on the floor.

"I guess we must have treated you right last night? Nice to see you back again."

Jane smiled. "We had such a good time, and I told my grandfather I'd love to come again sometime. They suggested tonight, and I said, why not?"

"Why not, indeed? So, when you're not gambling with

old men, what do you do?" He was flirting with her now and Jane had to admit, she was enjoying the attention. She'd hoped that taking extra care with her appearance might get his attention, and then she could see what she could learn, if anything. She knew it was really a longshot.

"I run a coffee shop, mostly takeout breakfast and lunch."

"You like to cook? I'm impressed."

"I do, actually. Baking, too."

"Maybe I'll have to stop in sometime and see for myself."

"What do you do when you're not organizing these parties?" Jane kept her tone light.

"Oh, I keep busy. I'm an investor in a few different businesses. Keeps me out of trouble," he said with a chuckle. She should have known he wouldn't say much. But still, she tried again.

"How long have you been having these parties? It's such a clever idea," she said and smiled at him, hoping to convey how impressed she was. He hesitated for a minute, but then the flattery worked and he answered the question.

"Almost five years now. We started small, just a party here and there, maybe once a month, if that. But it took off quickly and has really grown."

"That's wonderful! It feels just like a real casino, too."

"It is. We do everything a regular casino would do—we even give margin to our regular customers, so they can place bigger bets now and then if they are feeling lucky."

"Really? That's great. Though maybe not so great if they lose their bet?" She laughed lightly and Lanny chuckled, too. "Most of our regulars are experienced gamblers. They know the risks."

"I'd be much too nervous to ever do that," Jane admitted, hoping it made her sound like an inexperienced gambler.

Lanny smiled and looked amused. "How are the cards treating you tonight?" he asked.

"I got off to a good start, thought I knew what I was doing, and then everything fell apart. I thought it seemed like a good time to take a break."

"You're smart, then. When that happens, most people keep going, determined to get it back. But, it usually doesn't happen. That's what we count on."

Jane smiled. "The house always wins."

"Often enough, and it's a good thing or I wouldn't have a business." Someone waved at Lanny from across the room and he excused himself. "Duty calls. It was nice seeing you again. Good luck."

Lanny left and Jane made her way back to Gramps and Carl. They were both smiling and their stack of chips had grown.

"I'm killing it tonight," Carl said happily.

"I'm not doing too bad, either," Gramps said.

Jane settled in and started to play again. She lost two hands in a row, as did Gramps and Carl.

"That's it for me. I don't want to give any more of it back," Gramps said. He collected his chips and slid out of his seat.

"I'm done, too. You ready to go, Janie?" Carl asked.

"I'm ready."

After they cashed in their chips and headed for the door, Lanny caught up with them.

"Thanks for coming in. I hope to see you all again soon?" He addressed all of them, but was looking directly at Jane."

"I'm sure we'll be back soon," she said.

As they pulled out of the parking lot, Gramps spoke. "So, Lanny seems to have taken a shine to you. Did you learn anything?"

"No, he admitted that they sometimes will grant margin, loans for regular customers, but we pretty much already knew that."

"We'll keep digging. Something will turn up. It always does." Gramps was so optimistic. Jane had always liked that about him—though winning a few hundred dollars would put anyone in a good mood.

"We'll come back next Friday," Carl said. "Lanny seems to like you. Maybe you can keep talking to him."

Jane was curious to talk to Lanny some more. He was so charming and she had to admit she found him attractive, which was a little disturbing. From all accounts, Lanny was bad news. But it was hard for her to imagine him doing the kinds of things that were generally associated with the mob.

Gambling, sure, but harassing Samantha about a loan or potentially murdering someone? That didn't seem to fit the person she'd met. But, as she well knew, people were unpredictable, and capable of all kinds of things. She wasn't sure, though, that Lanny was their best lead. Her gut was telling her that there was something they were missing and that they needed to focus in a different direction.

22

The following Wednesday morning, Jane was trying out a new muffin recipe, toasted coconut and pineapple, and it looked like it was going to be a winner. She was taking them out of the oven when the front door chimed. She set the muffins on the counter to cool and went out front. It was still very early. Jane had only been open for about fifteen minutes and the morning rush didn't usually happen for another for-ty-five minutes or so.

"What smells so good?" Jake asked. He was standing at the counter, looking hungry.

"New muffin flavor, pineapple and toasted coconut. Want one? They're hot from the oven."

"How can I say no to that?"

"Coffee, too?"

"I'm good on coffee, thanks. I actually stopped in to see if you might be up for trivia tonight?"

That caught Jane by surprise. Before she could respond, he spoke again. "I thought we could sit at the bar this time. I hear that Chester and Maxine apparently like trivia. They were the first place winners last week."

"Really? Jane had been so surprised to see them together that it hadn't even occurred to her that they might have been there playing trivia.

"I was thinking—if you want to go that is—that we could sit at the bar this time, maybe near the two of them, if possible, and see if we can chat them up a bit."

"Do you really think either of them could be involved?" Jane knew they both had a motive, but she didn't think they had anything to do with it.

"I don't know if they did or didn't, but we have nothing else to go on, so we might as well keep talking to people."

"Okay, I'll play."

"Great, I'll be by at six." Jane watched him leave and was smiling to herself as Melissa walked in.

"Thanks for letting me come in a little late today. John always takes forever with my hair, but I love that he'll see me so early." She stopped and stared at Jane for a minute. "What are you looking so happy about?" Before Jane could even reply, she said, "That was Jake wasn't it? Do you have plans to go out again?"

"Sort of. We're going to trivia tonight at the pub."

Melissa raised her eyebrows. "A date?"

Jane sighed. "No, I don't think so. Not that I'd mind. It's just trivia. We have to defend our second place win from last week. And Jake is hoping that we see Chester and Maxine there and get a chance to talk to them."

"Okay. Well, it almost sounds like a date. Should be fun, anyway. Can't wait to hear about it tomorrow."

Later that afternoon when Jane was closing for the day, her cell phone rang and it was Nick.

"How's it going? Have you found the real murderer yet?" she teased him. He'd had the case all of a week now.

"Very funny. I have a favor to ask of you. Are you busy tomorrow night?"

"For what? I told you I'm not getting involved in this case."

"I know. I'm not asking you to. Not officially, anyway."

"What do you mean?"

"Drummond's stepson, Ben, is hosting a big company bash tomorrow night. It's a huge party the company throws every year for clients and friends. Drummond put us all on the guest list. I thought it might be fun for you. If you don't have other plans."

Damn him. Her schedule was clear and she was tempted.

"Why would Drummond put me on the guest list? I told him I won't work on this case already."

"Wishful thinking maybe? He values your opinion. We both do. The thinking is that we go to this party and just mingle. Maybe you get a chance to chat up Ben, see if you can learn anything." And this was part of the reason why Nick was good—he never gave up.

"Why don't you bring Liza? She's your investigator." The party did sound intriguing.

"I am bringing Liza. I thought we could all go, then go our separate ways and compare notes afterward."

Jane was silent for a moment, considering the idea. When she still didn't say anything, Nick pulled out his trump card. "The food is going to be really good. Lavender & Thyme is catering." They were one of the best caterers in the city. Nick knew her weakness.

"I wonder if they will make the lamb meatballs?" Jane said with a sigh. They were ridiculously delicious.

"So you'll go?"

"Yes, I'll go."

23

Jane got home around four thirty, fed Misty, and then jumped in the shower. An hour later, she was dressed and ready to go. Since they were going to the pub, she dressed casually—jeans and her favorite royal blue top. She still had a half-hour before Jake was due to arrive, so she made herself a cup of hot tea and sat down in her favorite chair in her living room. It was by a large window that had a distant view of the ocean.

As she took her first sip, Misty jumped up onto her lap and swished her tail in Jane's face, almost spilling her tea. She walked in a circle and then settled down and purred loudly while Jane petted her and thought about Maxine and Chester.

She hoped that they would be at trivia tonight and that she'd have a chance to chat with them. It still surprised her a bit that they seemed to be a couple. That implied that they'd been having an affair while Samantha and Chester were married.

But did Samantha know about it? Who else might have wanted Samantha dead? And why? Jane had no solid theories yet on any possible suspects. It didn't sound like Jake had uncovered any real evidence on anyone yet, either. But maybe he hadn't told her everything. Not yet, anyway.

At six o'clock sharp, there was a knock on the front door. Jane stood and Misty howled at the loss of her lap. "Sorry, sweetie," she said as the little cat strolled off, swishing her tail to indicate her displeasure.

Jane opened the door and Jake stood there, looking great and smelling even better. Jane didn't recall him wearing any cologne the last time they went out.

"Ready to go?" he asked.

"Yes, let me just get my jacket." Jane grabbed her lightweight jacket from the kitchen closet and they left. On the short drive to the pub, Jane asked if he'd learned anything new.

"Not a thing. I was hoping to have something more substantial by now, but I had to send my report off this morning, as is. The state police will be taking over now. I'll still be assisting them, of course."

"And you still want to solve it?" Jane knew she would have a hard time with that, just handing the case over and essentially giving up.

Jake grinned. "Of course I do. One of the reasons I came here was to get away from the constant grind of murders and crime in Boston, but handing a case over is something I don't think I'll ever get used to."

The pub looked busy, as usual, when Jake pulled into the parking lot. They went inside and while the restaurant was packed, there were quite a few open seats at the bar. Better still, Chester and Maxine were already there sitting at a corner, and there were empty seats next to them. Jake led the way and Jane sat next to Maxine with Jake on her right. Maxine smiled when she recognized her.

"How's your grandfather doing? Has he given any more thought to Riverhaven?"

Jane could see why Maxine did so well with real estate—she was on top of things. "I don't think he's ready to do anything yet. I'm not sure he ever will, to be honest. I think he was just humoring me by agreeing to get some information," she confessed.

Maxine smiled. "That's too bad. I understand, though. If anything changes, please let me know."

"Of course. Are you playing trivia tonight? Jake and I were here last week and it was fun."

"Yes, it's become a regular thing with us." Maxine took a sip of her beer and then said, "We actually won last week. First time for that. Chester knew the answer to the last question and that did it for us." For the final question, players were able to wager any amount up to their total score, so it was possible, even if you were in last place, to still win, depending on how that last question went for everyone.

"That's great!" Jane said and then turned her attention to the bartender, a fifty-something woman named Donna, who came over to take their drink order. She had been working at the pub for what seemed like forever, and was one of her grandfather's favorite people. Jane and Jake both ordered draft beers, an IPA made by a local brewery.

"Your grandfather was in last night. Told me he'd run away with me, whenever I was ready," she chuckled.

"That sounds like Gramps." Her grandfather loved to flirt with all the waitresses and bartenders at the pub. "Was David with him?"

"Yes, they both had the Fenway."

Her grandfather and cousin David had a standing pizza date. Just about every week, they came for buy-one-get-one pizza at the pub.

"Pizza?" Jake asked as Donna handed them menus.

"Definitely." They discussed what kind to get and settled on the Fenway, too, which was sausage, pepper and onion, named after Fenway Park, home of the Boston Red Sox.

As they sipped their beers and waited for their pizza, Jane filled him in on her latest trip to Mumford.

"So, you talked to Lanny? But you don't think he's involved?" he asked and looked somewhat surprised.

Jane hesitated before saying, "Well, I don't know for sure, of course. But, he was just so friendly. It was hard to picture him harassing Samantha, let alone killing her."

Jake raised his eyebrows. "Ted Bundy was handsome, and charming."

"That's true." He did have a point. Ted Bundy was one of the all-time worst serial killers.

"I've heard he's a good-looking guy and that the ladies seem to like him. That doesn't mean he's not dangerous. Lanny's in the Irish mob. He's not a good guy," Jake insisted.

"I suppose," Jane agreed reluctantly. Intellectually, she knew that Jake was right, but she'd found Lanny so likable and attractive. Not that she was interested—she wasn't. But, she could still appreciate and enjoy the attention of a charming, attractive man.

Maxine and Chester had ordered pizza, too. Theirs smelled delicious when Donna set it down in front of them, and Jane's stomach growled. She didn't have to wait long, though. A few minutes later, their pizzas arrived, too, and they dug in. Trivia started just as they finished eating and for the next hour, they had fun playing. There was always a break halfway through the game and that's when Jane tried to talk to Maxine again.

"How'd the first half go for you?" she asked.

"So-so. I don't expect we'll have a repeat performance of last week unless we have an amazing second half. What about you two?"

"We did okay. It really all comes down to the last question I think?"

"So true," Maxine agreed and then a moment later said, "You know, it just occurred to me. You run that coffee right? Comfort something or other?"

"Yes, Comfort & Joy."

"Well, I don't know if you've thought of expanding, but Chester has decided to sell the B & B. I just put the listing up today."

That was a surprise. "Really? I hadn't been thinking about expanding. Why is he selling?"

Chester heard the question and leaned forward to answer. "It's too much work. I just don't have time for it."

"But, I thought you and Samantha were fighting over it?"

Chester chuckled. "That's what people do when they get divorced. Neither wants to give anything up."

"What are you asking for it?" Jane asked out of curiosity.

Maxine mentioned a figure that almost caused Jane's jaw to drop.

"That's a bit too rich for my blood," she said with a smile. She never would have guessed that the B & B was worth so much.

"It's a really good price," Maxine insisted. "We priced it for a quick sale."

The 'we' caught Jane's attention. Was she referring to the two of them as a couple? Or was she just talking in her capacity as a realtor?

"What will you do when it sells?" Jane asked. She wondered if Chester was planning on leaving the area.

"We are going to take one heck of a vacation," Chester said with a smile. "Then, we were thinking of maybe buying a place in Florida."

"That's nice. Will you be moving there, then? Or just a second home?"

"We're not sure," Maxine answered, which surprised Jane.

"Have the two of you been dating long?" Jane asked.

"It's been what, about three months, honey?" Maxine asked Chester, who immediately shot her a warning look.

"Oh, silly me, three weeks. We've just been friends forever, though."

"Of course. Well, a trip and a Florida house sounds wonderful to me." She glanced at Jake who had been listening to the exchange with interest and then added, "I have to admit, I wish I was in a position to be able to buy the B & B. It would go well with the shop."

Maxine's eyes lit up. "There's all kinds of loan programs available, you know."

Jane smiled. "I know. I got one when I opened Comfort & Joy. It hasn't even been a year yet, so I can't imagine they'd consider giving me that much more money. In a few years, maybe."

"Ah, well, if you think of anyone, please send them my way."

"I'll do that."

The second half started, and Jane and Jake both ordered another beer and focused on the game again. As before, it came down to the final question and once again they came in second place, though first place went to a different team this time.

"Congrats on second place!" Maxine said as Chester reached for their bill. Everyone seemed to clear out of the pub as soon as trivia ended and they were no exception. Jake had already asked for and paid the bill, refusing, once again to let Jane contribute.

"Maybe you can treat next time," he said as they walked out to the car.

"I won't come again, unless you let me," Jane said with a smile, and she meant it.

Once they were in the car and buckled up, Jake started the engine and as they drove off, Jane asked, "So what did you think of the conversation in there?"

"I'm not sure. Obviously, the two of them started their

relationship long before Samantha died. But does mean they had anything to do with her death? I didn't hear anything to suggest that."

"I didn't, either. They're definitely guilty of cheating, but does that mean they killed her? It seems like a reach to me, and we don't have any kind of evidence to tie either of them to it."

"We'll just have to keep digging until we uncover something that will tie someone to it," Jake said. "Piece of cake, right?

Jane chuckled. "Right." As Jake pulled into the driveway, she said, "I could actually go for a piece of cake. Would you like one?"

"You have cake?"

"I always have cake. I'm often testing new recipes at home, then make them for customers in the shop. Do you like chocolate?"

"Who doesn't?"

"I have a double-chocolate fudge cake with orange cream frosting."

"I'm in," Jake said as he parked and cut the engine.

They went in and Misty came running to greet them. But once she saw Jake and realized that Jane had company, she turned around and walked away with her tail held high.

"She's a bit of a snob," Jane apologized as Jake came into the kitchen and took a seat at the small island counter while Jane got the cake out of the refrigerator. She sliced two pieces and then slid one to him.

Jake took a big bite and then said nothing. Nothing at all,

until he reached for a second bite and said, "This is amazing. Amazing!"

"Thanks." Jane took a bite of her piece and smiled. She had to agree with his assessment. It was an excellent cake.

"Do you want coffee or tea or something else with it?" she offered.

Jake had practically licked his plate clean. It was spotless.

"No, I'm good. I should head out. Big day tomorrow."

"Oh, okay." Jane walked him to the front door and he looked like he was going to say goodbye, but instead he pulled her toward him, leaned over and gave her a quick, firm kiss on the lips. Then he grinned.

"Good night, Jane."

Jane simply nodded, feeling in a bit of a daze because he completely took her by surprise. She hadn't seen a kiss coming at all.

Misty reappeared and rubbed against her leg, meowing loudly for attention. Jane reached down to pet her and muttered to herself, "I guess it was a date."

24

S o it was a date!" Melissa exclaimed after Jane filled her
in the next morning at the shop. It was very early, before
they opened and the two of them were in the kitchen cooking
and baking for the day ahead.

"I'm not so sure about that. But I certainly wouldn't mind
if it was," Jane said with a smile. She'd smiled to herself more
than once since Jake left the night before. She'd always been
attracted to Jake, but didn't think he'd ever really noticed her
that way. She also realized that Jake must have completely
ruled her out as a possible suspect as well, which was a relief.
Plus, he wasn't officially heading up the investigation anymore, so maybe that's why he did it. She was just glad that he
did, and hoped that it could be the start of something.

"What are you up to tonight?" Melissa asked. "Did Jake
ask you out again?"

Jane frowned for a moment. "No, he didn't mention anything about going out again."

"Oh, no worries. I'm sure he will. I'm thinking about going to the movies tonight, to see that new romantic comedy. You want to join me?"

"I'd love to, but I told Nick I'd go to a party with him." It had sounded intriguing when he mentioned it the other day, especially if lamb meatballs might be involved, but Jane was no longer all that eager to go. Even though Boston was less than twenty miles away, it still usually took at least forty-five minutes to get there because of traffic, sometimes even longer. Going there on a weeknight made for a long day, considering how early she had to be up.

"Where is it at?" Melissa asked.

"At the Top of the Hub, one of the large function rooms at the Skywalk Observatory."

"I had dinner once at the Top of the Hub. The views were amazing." Jane had been there once for dinner, too, when she and Nick were dating. The restaurant was on the top floor of the Prudential Center, one of the landmark buildings in Boston and one of the tallest, with fifty-two floors.

"I'm sure it will be fun," Jane said. She would just have to get a second wind, maybe have an extra cup of coffee before she left for the day.

"Are you and Nick getting back together?" Melissa asked. She looked confused and given what Jane had just said about Jake, she couldn't blame her.

"No, it's not a date. It's a work thing for him and I'm just doing him a favor by going. He wants my opinion on a case he's working on. There's some people there he wants me to talk to."

"Oh, okay, then. Good." Melissa smiled and then added, "I like you and Jake together."

Soon after they opened, Gramps, Carl and Eddie came in for their usual coffees and muffins. Once they were all seated, Gramps came back to the counter and waited until Janie finished serving a customer. There was no one else waiting in line at the moment and Gramps looked excited about something.

"Janie, you busy right after work today?" he asked.

"I'm busy later tonight, but I'm free right after work. What's up?"

"I'm taking you for a ride. There's something you gotta see."

"What is it?'

"You'll see. I'll fill you in later. You're too busy now," he said as a group of customers walked in.

"Well, you're certainly being mysterious, but okay. I'll be ready to go at four o'clock."

"I'll be here."

At four o'clock sharp, Gramps walked in the front door.

"Ready to go?" He had a gleam in his eye.

"I'm ready." Jane locked the door behind her and followed Gramps to his car and climbed in.

"So, on the way over this morning, I saw something interesting. I took the scenic route, to change things up a bit, and drove along the waterfront. I noticed a new house going up. Looks like it's going to be a big one, right on the water. I slowed down to get a good look and saw something that surprised the heck out of me."

"What's that?"

"That Chester guy, Maxine and Lanny were all there together. They were looking at the house and Maxine was writing something down. Then they walked along the edge of the foundation, all around the house. Looked like they were in deep conversation about something. Made my something-is-off radar go on."

"Interesting that they know Lanny," Janie said, wondering what the significance of that relationship was, if anything.

"Here it is. Looks like it is going to be a beauty. Location can't be beat, anyway." Gramps slowed the car to a stop. No one was there, so he pulled into the driveway.

"Let's check it out." Gramps was out of the car before Jane could even respond. She got out of the car and walked over to where he was standing, looking out at the sea. The property looked like it would be impressive. There was nothing there but the foundation, but it was large and the lot was oversized and lovely, sloping down to the ocean. It was a corner lot, so most of the rooms would have water views.

He walked over to a stake in the ground that had a permit nailed to it. They both leaned in to get a closer look. The owners were listed as both Maxine Underwood and Chester Sellers and the construction company was Chester's.

"So they're building a house together. That's pretty serious, and expensive. No wonder Chester wants to sell the B & B. This can't be cheap."

"Maybe Samantha's life insurance policy was bigger than we thought?" Gramps wondered.

"But where does Lanny figure into this?" Strange that he knows them. Maybe one of his businesses is real estate or construction related." Jane said.

"So, it might not mean much of anything. But, I thought it was kind of interesting. Especially when I saw the three of them together," Gramps said as they walked back to the car.

"It is kind of strange. Neither one of them seem to be grieving much for Samantha," Jane commented.

"We're on for tomorrow night, right?" Gramps asked as they drove off.

"Gambling in Mumford? Yes, I'm actually looking forward to it." Jane had to admit she enjoyed playing blackjack, and she was most curious to talk to Lanny again and see if she could find out a bit more about his other businesses.

"Good, because Carl has been talking about it all week. I think he enjoys it a little too much, if you know what I mean."

"We'll keep an eye on him. You can cut him off if he gets out of hand."

"Oh, you can count on that," Gramps said with a chuckle.

25

Jane stared at her closet, willing the perfect outfit to reveal itself. Finally, she settled on her go-to fancy dress. It was a classic, little black dress, sleeveless, with an elegant boat-neck and low-cut in the back. It was cocktail length and slimming as it hugged her body and made her waist look smaller. She paired it with black patent leather, open-toed heels, a tennis bracelet and diamond stud earrings that her mother had given her for her college graduation years ago. She blew her hair straight, kept her makeup simple except for a fire-engine red lipstick, a color that made her feel happy.

She drove into Boston and parked at the Prudential Center parking garage. Nick had said they would meet for a drink first at the Top of Hub bar and then go to the party on the SkyWalk. When she walked into the bar, Nick was already there, sipping a dirty martini and gazing around the room. He smiled when he saw her and she walked over and gave him a hug.

"You look fantastic," he said appreciatively.

He looked good himself, as he always did. Nick wore a business suit well. Today, he was in charcoal gray with a red tie and crisp, white shirt.

"So do you. Where's Liza?"

"She should be here any minute. Have you met Ben before? I'll be sure to introduce you as soon as I see him."

"No, I haven't had the pleasure. Does he know that his stepfather is having him and his brother investigated?"

Nick shook his head. "No, all he knows is that I agreed to take on his father's case, and to file an appeal. He said he'll do whatever he can to help." He raised his eyebrows at that.

"What, you don't think he's sincere?"

"Just wait until you meet him. Let's just say the apple doesn't seem to fall far from the tree. The only question is who is more of a criminal, him or his brother?"

"You don't think Alex Drummond is just blowing smoke? He really thinks one of his sons was behind those murders?"

"He really does. He made it sound quite reasonable, actually."

"He's a good salesman," Jane agreed.

"Liza's here!" Nick said. Jane turned to see Liza Armstrong making her way toward them. Jane liked Liza. They had worked together a few times on bigger cases. The older woman was very thorough and analytical. She didn't miss much. She had learned a few things from Liza during her time with the firm.

"Jane, it's so great to see you!" Liza gave her a big hug.

"Liza, what are you drinking?" Nick asked.

"Um, a cosmo I guess," Liza said, and a minute later, the bartender handed her a pretty, pink martini.

"Ladies, shall we?" Nick led the way to the SkyWalk Observatory and the large function room where the party was being held.

The room was already buzzing when they walked in. Moments later, a server came by with a tray of beef wellington bites and they all took one. A few more servers came by with appetizers as they stood near a window, admiring the breathtaking, wraparound view of Boston. From their vantage point, they could see all of the Back Bay and from the Commons and Public Gardens to the financial district, Boston Harbor and the airport beyond. It was dizzying, being so high up and seeing so much.

Jane took a step back from the edge. They were fully glassed-in, but looking out and then down was a bit intimidating. Jane had always had a fear of heights.

"Here he comes. I'll introduce you both," Nick said as a tall, good-looking man who appeared to be in his mid-thirties walked towards them. He had sandy hair and a clean-cut, preppy look about him.

"Nick, glad you could make it," Ben said warmly and smiled at their small group.

"Ben, these two lovely ladies work with me, Liza and Jane."

Jane shot him a look and he immediately corrected himself. "Or rather, Jane used to work with me. I guess I'm still hoping she might change her mind and come back someday."

"One can always hope, right?" Ben said and laughed.

"It's nice to meet you," Liza and Jane said at the same time.

"You, as well. I hope I have a chance to chat further with you later." He was looking at Jane as he spoke. "But right now, duty calls. If you'll excuse me..." And he was off.

"So, what did you think?" Nick asked.

"He seems pleasant enough, and is certainly a good dresser. Other than that, I won't really know until I talk to him further," Jane said.

"That was a sharp suit," Nick said, and Jane smiled. Nick was terribly vain and she knew it needled him that she'd commented on Ben's clothing.

"I thought he seemed a bit nervous," Liza said thoughtfully. "Did you happen to notice his hand, the one that wasn't holding a drink, was shaking a little? Maybe he doesn't enjoy large gatherings like this, or something is stressing him out."

Jane was impressed. "I didn't notice that, Liza. Thanks. I'll pay closer attention if I get a chance to chat with him again later."

"Ladies, it looks like my glass had a hole in it," Nick joked. "I'm going to head to the bar. Can I get either of you something?" Liza still had a full drink, but Jane was nearly done with her wine.

"I'll have another, thanks."

When Nick returned with their drinks they strolled through the crowd, making their way around the room, which wrapped halfway around the building. When they reached the other side, they could see past Fenway Park, the Charles River, and Cambridge and beyond. Jane took care not to get too close to the edge. She didn't dare look down again.

Nick knew a few people there and wandered off to mingle, while Jane and Liza stayed to themselves, catching up and trying all the delicious appetizers as they passed by. Their spot was near where the servers went into the kitchen, so they had first crack at everything new as it came out.

"I think we picked the best spot," Liza chuckled as another server stopped to offer them the lamb meatballs Jane had been craving. They were spiced and served with a yogurt dipping sauce of some kind. The flavors were outstanding.

"Yes, we did," Jane agreed as she reached for a second meatball.

"We probably should try and mingle eventually, I suppose," Liza said reluctantly.

"When we're both ready for another drink, we can head in opposite directions, each going to a different bar and see who we might run into. I think we might have better luck, actually, talking to people if we're alone."

"I agree. I'm just about ready, if you are." Liza downed the last sip of her drink, and Jane didn't have much left in her glass.

"I'm ready. I'll meet you back here in a bit."

Liza wandered off and Jane did the same, slowly making her way through the crowd. As she reached the bar, she stopped short when she saw a familiar and unexpected face. Lanny was there. He smiled when he saw her and walked her way. She supposed it shouldn't be a surprise that he was here. He was a stockholder, after all, but she'd separated the two of them in her mind, and was focused solely on talking to Ben.

"Well, I'm seeing a lot of you lately," he said as he reached her. "What brings you here?"

"A former colleague invited me to come tonight," she said.

"Oh, who's that?"

"Nick Dawson."

Something flashed across his eyes, and then they narrowed a bit, "You're here with Nick? I didn't realize he was coming."

"Your brother invited him. He's working on your father's appeal."

"Right, of course." Lanny's response was smooth and he didn't miss a beat, but Jane could see him wondering why Nick was there and, more importantly, why she was with him.

"We're good friends, even though I don't work with him any longer," she explained, hoping he might think it was more of a date than it actually was.

He seemed to relax a bit at that, and changed the subject.

"So, will I see you again in Mumford? Or have you scratched your gambling itch?"

Jane chuckled. "Yes, I think you will see me soon. I'd forgotten how much I love playing blackjack, and my grandfather and Carl are thrilled that they have someone else to go along with them. Gives them an excuse to go, I think."

They really were tickled that she was so interested in accompanying them, though her grandfather did worry a bit about Carl. He was concerned that he could get carried away with his gambling, if he didn't have people with him to shut him down before he got into trouble.

"I was surprised to see you here," Jane admitted.

He raised his eyebrows at that. "Really? My brother helps my stepfather run this company, but we're both major stock holders. I'm not actively involved with the day-to-day running of the company the way that Ben is, but I am very much aware of what is going on," he said and took a sip of his drink, which looked like either a scotch or whiskey on the rocks. He smiled and then added, "In spite of everything, we're having our best year. Thanks to the new release, sales and profits are up."

"That's great. I'm surprised that you don't work at the company as well," Jane commented.

"My talents and interests lie elsewhere. Besides, I think my brother and I might kill each other if we had to work together all the time. It's better this way."

"He's right about that," said a voice behind them.

Jane turned and Ben was there.

"Jane, have you met my brother, Ben, yet?" Lanny asked.

"Nick introduced us earlier," Ben said. He then glanced at Lanny and then Jane before adding, "Nick brought his two best investigators with him."

"Really?" The wariness was back in Lanny's eyes.

"Former investigator. We don't work together any longer and no matter what Nick thinks, I've told him I have no interest in coming back to work at the firm. I like what I'm doing now."

"Right, he said you're running a coffee shop in a small town or something like that?" Ben asked.

"Yes, a breakfast and lunch place, mostly takeout, in Waverly. I love it."

Both of them looked at her in disbelief.

"I'll take your word on that, but it sounds like hard work to me," Ben said.

"Of course it does. You can't cook," Lanny teased him.

"Well, yes, there is that," Ben admitted and then grinned.

Lanny's cell phone vibrated then and he checked to see who was calling. "I'm sorry, I need to take this. Excuse me."

He wandered off and Ben looked at her empty glass. "It looks like you were on your way to the bar. What are you drinking?"

"Chardonnay."

"Hold on, I'll be right back." He walked over to the bar, and moments later returned with a new glass of wine.

"So, you really don't miss investigating? I think I remember my father saying he'd wished you were on his side during the trial."

"I do miss it a little," she admitted. "But not enough to go back into it. I've moved on and I'm really happy now. Cooking was always a dream I had."

"I can understand that. I'm following my dream, as well. We're in striking distance of completely dominating our market."

"I thought you were already the leader, that this new product release pushed you to number one?"

"Yes, and that's been exciting to watch. But that's just one product. We have two more releasing over the next two years and that's when we should really own the marketplace and the stock price should reflect it." His naked ambition was plain to see.

"That's exciting. How do you stay ahead of your competitors?"

"It's not easy. We have some tough competition. But we're scrappy, and resourceful. We basically do whatever it takes to give us a competitive edge. We have the best and most motivated development team and our sales guys are hungry. When we have all the right pieces in place, it becomes a perfect storm of momentum. Impossible to stop." He grinned and added, "At least, that's the goal."

Jane was impressed with his drive. Ben had an intensity that was fascinating. In their own ways, each brother seemed to have all the ingredients to be successful. Was Ben so competitive that he'd cross the line to give himself an illegal advantage? Jane wasn't sure. Like his brother, he was somewhat hard to read. Both men were clearly intelligent. But was either one of them a killer?

A beautiful blonde woman came up to Ben and whispered something in his ear. He blushed a bit and then said, "I'm afraid I'm being summoned. Someone is waiting to talk to me. If you'll excuse me."

"Of course," Jane said and watched as the two of them wandered off. Jane strolled away herself and as she came around a corner, she stopped short as she recognized a familiar voice. Lanny was talking to someone and when she heard the name Maxine, she froze in her spot and took a sip of her wine, listening intently.

"I just don't know if building that new house is such a good idea right now. I know. I'm just saying maybe wait a while, until this all blows over. They'll turn their focus to something else. They always do. Right. Okay, talk to Chester, see what you can do." He stopped talking then and Jane spun around and quickly walked back to where she'd been before, so she wouldn't run into Lanny right after he got off his call.

What she'd overheard, though, was concerning. Why did Lanny care so much about the house Maxine and Chester were building? Why the advice to hold off for a while? What was his connection to Maxine?

Jane found Liza near the bar, gazing out the window.

"Did you learn anything?" she asked when she saw Jane.

"I'm not sure," Jane admitted. Nick appeared just then as well and also asked, "Any luck?"

"Well, I'm not sure if it's relevant to your case, but I did overhear a phone conversation of Lanny's. It may be relevant to the murder of the woman that was found at my shop." She told them what she'd heard Lanny say to Maxine.

"It just doesn't make much sense why he'd warn her to keep a low profile, unless there was a reason for it and that he might somehow be involved."

"Do you think she may have hired Lanny to kill the woman?" Liza asked, quickly connecting the same dots that Jane had.

"I think it's possible, or that Chester did and Maxine knows about it."

"Do you think you've heard enough to justify poking around online now?" Nick asked. It was what Jane had been thinking about ever since she'd heard the tail end of Lanny's call.

"I think so. Depending on what I find, I'll see if I can expand the search to see if anything relevant turns up for you, as well."

"I'd appreciate that," Nick said.

"I wish I understood how you do what you do with those computers," Liza said in admiration.

"I can't guarantee that it will work, or that I'll find anything, but I'll let you know if I do."

"Liza, did you get a chance to talk to Ben?" Nick asked.

"I did. He's a smart young man. Perhaps a bit too smart. He asked quite a few questions about what I do at the firm. I answered them honestly, of course, but giving as little information as possible. But still, it was enough to make him nervous. Especially when he realized that you brought two investigators here tonight."

"I had a similar conversation," Jane said. "But, I assured him that I am not returning to investigative work."

"Never say never," Nick said with a grin. "I'm fine with you consulting like this every now and then."

"I'm not consulting for you," Jane said automatically. Then she thought about it for a moment and chuckled, "Okay, I guess I sort of am. Unofficially, anyway."

"We can make it official anytime you like," Nick pressed.

"I'll keep that in mind," Jane said with a smile.

26

When Jane finished up work the next day, she drove by Maxine's real estate office and was happy to see that her car was there. The office was located in a strip mall, so Jane parked out of the direct sight of the office, but facing the front door so she could see who was coming and going. She turned off her car engine, set up her laptop and used her sniffing software to search out the real estate office's network.

She was hoping that there was a chance that it was unsecured, as that would make her search much easier. She remembered her saying something about hating technology, so thought there might be a possibility that she didn't want to bother with passwords.

She was right. Her software dinged that the connection had been made, and from there it was fairly simple for Jane to access and search her email. Within minutes, she crossed another hurdle when she found a folder marked 'passwords'. It wasn't always this easy. Jane was prepared to dig deeper and she had the technical know-how to do it, but more often than not, her coding skills were unnecessary. Creative searching often led her to what she needed.

She clicked the folder open and grinned. All of Maxine's passwords were there. She jotted down the one she was most interested in, in case she lost her connection, and then she quickly searched her email for a combination of different words, anything that would be some kind of a trail to Lanny or Samantha.

She searched their names and scrolled through any emails, though there were no emails from Lanny, just Chester and Samantha. But, there was nothing incriminating in any of them. Maxine was smart enough not to put anything in writing in an email. Jane decided to do her next search at home, now that she had the passwords she needed.

Ten minutes later, she was home. She gave Misty some attention, fed her and then went upstairs to her home office and turned on her desktop computer. She looked up Maxine's bank and then entered her email and password info. Once she was in, she started to look through her recent transactions, starting with the current week and then working backwards to a month before Samantha died. Very quickly, she found what she was looking for.

She noted a large check to Chester's construction company, and a few days after Samantha's death, there was another large check to the Mercedes dealership. But there was a transaction two weeks before Samantha's murder that got her attention. A check for fifty thousand dollars was debited from the account. Jane clicked on the check icon to see the image of the check and it was made out to a company called Unlimited Freedom, LLC. And in the memo field, she had written 'services'.

She was unfamiliar with Unlimited Freedom, LLC., but had a feeling she knew who might be behind it. A few more searches and she found the database registration that listed the principals attached to Unlimited Freedom, LLC. There was just one person. Landon Drummond.

27

Jane's next call was to Jake and he was impressed with what she'd discovered.

"Okay, let me share this with the state guys. They'll have to do their own discovery, of course, but since both Maxine and Chester benefited from Samantha's death, we should be able to get a warrant to search basic records, bank accounts, laptops, things like that."

"We were going to go to Mumford tonight. Gramps and Carl were looking forward to it. When will this happen? I wouldn't want Lanny to get of wind of it while we are there."

Jake thought for a moment. "It's almost five now. I'll write my request up and submit it first thing in the morning. It will probably take them a week to actually subpoena the records, so you should be fine to go tonight."

"Okay, we'll go, then. I also told Lanny last night that we were coming, so he is expecting us."

"Be careful," Jake warned.

"We will," Jane assured him.

Friday night's party was held on Holly Lane in Mumford. This time, it was in the basement of a men's gym and the lovely smell of sweat greeted them as they walked inside.

"Not quite as plush as the last place," Gramps joked as Evan, the bouncer, checked them in. He now knew all their names and wished them luck.

"I'm telling you, the service here keeps getting better," Carl said with a chuckle.

"Right, as long as Janie is with us. She's our lucky charm," Gramps agreed.

"I don't know about that," Jane said. She'd dressed a little more casually this time, with a more modest white v-neck sweater, jeans, and a pair of brown and pink, cowboy boots.

They arrived a little later than usual because Carl had a chiropractor appointment that afternoon, so when they made their way downstairs, the room was already packed with people. But, as he always managed to do, Carl's eagle eyes spotted the one table that had three open seats and he made a beeline for it.

They settled in and played for a solid hour before Jane caught a glimpse of Lanny. He came in and went straight for the bar, taking his usual position at the far end where he could lean against the bar and watch the room. Jane wasn't as eager to talk to him, now that she was fairly sure he was involved with Samantha's murder. Her instinct was to stay far away. But still, she was curious to see what, if anything, he might have to say.

"I'll be back in a few minutes," she said, and eased herself off her seat and made her way to the bar. She ordered a glass of wine and sat there for a moment sipping it. Lanny caught her eye and nodded hello, but didn't come over to talk to her. He was frowning and looked like he was in a bad mood. She was about to take her drink back to the table, figuring that Lanny wasn't in a social mood, when suddenly he was right next to her.

"You did come. I wasn't sure if you still would," he said cryptically.

"Yes. As I mentioned, they really wanted to come and insisted I go with them."

"That's nice." His cell phone buzzed and his face grew stormy when he saw who was calling.

"Did you take care of it?" he barked into the phone, followed by, "I don't care what his excuses are. We had a deal. He knows what the consequences are. Just handle it." He slammed the phone down on the bar when he hung up and then turned to Jane and apologized. "I'm sorry. I don't usually lose my cool like that."

Jane was shocked at his behavior, but simply stayed calm and said, "Rough day?"

He chuckled. "Something like that. I'd love to stay and chat, but I have to go talk to someone. Maybe I'll catch up with you later. Good luck."

"Thanks." Jane took her drink back to the table and said softly to both Gramps and Carl, "I'm ready to go whenever you two are."

They looked at her in surprise and then Gramps said, "We'll go right after this hand. Right, Carl?"

"But I am in the middle of a winning streak!" Carl protested.

"Janie wants to go Carl. So we're going."

"Fine."

Both Carl and Gramps won their hands, which made Carl happy, but he was still muttering about leaving too early as they walked outside and got into the car.

"I'm sorry, Carl, I just got a bad feeling after talking with Lanny. He's in a funny mood. Things don't seem to be going his way today and I sense that he has a bit of a temper. I thought it best for us to leave, especially given what I found out earlier. I was on the fence about whether or not to share it with you both yet, but I think it's best if I do." She went on to tell them what she'd discovered earlier and confirmed with her searches.

"I gave Jake the information before we came here tonight and he's sending it off to be investigated tomorrow morning."

"So, it doesn't look good for Maxine or Lanny, or even Chester. He must have known, too, I imagine," Gramps said.

"I'd be very surprised if he didn't know," Jane agreed.

"You know, I meant to mention this earlier and it slipped by mind. I've been doing some asking around, too, and you know the good Judy? Well, we had lunch at the 99 yesterday and we were chatting about this and she said she remembered that Chester and Maxine were once high school sweethearts. They got in a tiff one summer, broke up and Chester was out one night drinking, trying to get over Maxine, and met Samantha. They hooked up and it was just a fling for him, but she got pregnant, and he did the honorable thing."

"But they don't have any kids." Jane said.

"Supposedly, she lost the baby. If there ever was a baby," Gramps said cynically.

"Odd, then, that she and Maxine were such good friends," Jane said.

"Samantha didn't know about Maxine until years later. Neither Maxine nor Chester ever said anything to her, and she and Maxine met in a yoga class and hit it off. Eventually, she found out. Her marriage to Chester was never a good one. They were never really in love, though she was always more in love with him. She made Maxine her beneficiary and told her she owed her, because she did feel guilty for stealing Chester away, even though she never did it intentionally."

"So why did they kill her, then?" Jane asked.

"Greed and hatred would be my guess," Gramps said. "Maxine was friendly with Samantha, but always resented her for taking Chester away. By killing her, she gets every-thing. Chester and all of Samantha's assets. I suspect she felt she was due, for not having Chester all those years."

"Maybe. But did Chester know?"

"Chester is no angel. I'd be very surprised if he didn't know, though it's certainly possible." Gramps said as they pulled up to Janie's door.

"Thanks. I'll keep you posted," Jane said as she got out of the car.

"You'd better!" Gramps said with a chuckle.

28

Jane, can you help us out?" Jake asked. He'd stopped into the Comfort & Joy and pulled Jane aside for a moment and filled her in. The computer team for the state police had found the same information that Jane did and they were ready to act, but they wanted to kill a few birds with one stone.

"So, we'd like to arrest Lanny and shut down the Mumford operation at the same time. If you, your grandfather and Carl could go like you normally do and then text us to come in, we'll be waiting outside. At the same time, we'll have another team bring Chester and Maxine in." They had dug even deeper and found something that connected Chester, as well. It turned out that he also had a fifty thousand dollar payment to Lanny's company on the same date, and the police theorized that they shared the cost of the hit equally.

"Okay. My grandfather and Carl will love this," Janie said.

"Well, be careful, Janie. I'm not convinced this is the best approach, but they really want to shut the Mumford gambling down."

"We'll be careful," Janie assured him.

"Look a little less excited, both of you," Janie said as they walked into the function hall on Smith Road in Mumford. This time, the event was being held on the second floor. Evan was happy as ever to see them and this time, they'd arrived a little earlier than usual. Jane was the most nervous of the bunch.

She knew that by now, Lanny was aware that both Maxine and Chester were under investigation and that their records had been subpoenaed. She wasn't even sure if he'd be in because of it. But an hour later, he was in his usual position at the bar, glowering at the room.

She supposed that he probably felt safe here as the police were unaware of the Mumford locations. Jane waited a few minutes and then told Gramps she was going for a glass of wine. They'd discussed the plan earlier. She was to go to the bar and hopefully talk to Lanny, and after about five minutes, Gramps was to send a text message to Jake, giving them the green light to come in.

Jane ordered her drink and glanced Lanny's way. He was staring at her, his face unsmiling. She took a sip of her wine and waited. He came over to her finally and sat next to her.

"It was you, wasn't it?" he asked, looking at her intently.

"I'm not sure what you're talking about," she said. She

wasn't surprised that he'd figured out that she was involved. He'd been wary when he saw her at the company party, and no doubt Maxine and Chester had called and filled him in as soon as they were arrested.

"I think you know. It makes sense. It's what you do. Investigate, even when you don't really do it anymore. I'm not stupid, you know."

"No, you're not. You strike me as pretty smart, actually. So I wondered why you'd do it? You don't need to."

Lanny smiled, then leaned over and lightly ran his hands along the side of Jane's chest and across her back. When he was apparently satisfied that she wasn't wearing a wire, he said, "No, I don't need to. It might shock you, but I do it because I want to. It's a business transaction. I make other people's problems disappear, and I'm very good at it."

Jane was shocked, but then collected herself and asked the question that she was really dying to know. "What was up with that note? 'I took care of her for you?'"

Lanny chuckled. "Oh, I had a little fun with that. We talked about how to kill her and how to dispose of the body and it just seemed perfect to leave it by your trash, given that you had more of an obvious motive than anyone, it seemed, given her antagonistic attitude toward you and the lawsuit. I added that note just to stir things up and make it seem like maybe you had hired someone or at least that someone else was involved. I thought it was rather clever, actually."

"Not that clever, unfortunately. For you, that is," Jane said as there was a commotion downstairs and then suddenly a team of police burst into the room and told everyone to freeze. Lanny jumped up and ran, but they were ready for him and the closest policeman hit him with a Taser and then threw cuffs on him.

"Everyone out, and down to the station. We'll need statements from everyone here."

"I guess that means we don't get to cash in before we leave?" Carl asked.

"Carl, it's time to go," Gramps said. "Janie?"

"Right behind you."

29

The following Monday, Jane had just put a second batch of toasted coconut and pineapple muffins in the oven when the front door chimed and Jake walked in. It was early. Jane had just unlocked the front door and Melissa had arrived only a few minutes before and was tying on her apron as she walked to the register.

"Do you have any of those pineapple muffins ready yet?" Jake asked when he reached the counter.

"Sure do. Just put a second batch in the oven, because they've been selling out every day. Coffee, too?"

"Medium, black. Thanks." Jake paid and then said, "Can we talk for a minute?" Melissa was standing right there, so Jane guessed he meant privately.

"Sure. Melis, I'll be right back." She walked to the back of the shop and sat at a small corner table. Jake settled into the seat across from her and took a sip of his coffee.

"I just wanted to thank you again for helping, especially with Lanny. They've been wanting to shut down that Mumford gambling ring and the group that Lanny was involved with for a long time. He was into a lot more than just gambling, as you probably gathered from his involvement with Maxine and Chester."

"I'm not surprised to hear it. I thought he was so charming at first, that a little harmless gambling might be the extent of it, but I saw a very different side of him at the end. It's a shame, because he's smart, like his brother. He could have gone far in a legitimate business."

"How's that investigation going?" Jake asked. "Have either Lanny or his brother been tied to those murders?"

"Not yet, though it looks as though Lanny is probably involved. They're still not sure about his brother. There's a lot of investigating left to do there."

"You won't be the one doing the digging, I hope?" Jake looked at her intently and she appreciated his concern.

"No. I don't plan to be involved any further with the Drummond case. I just want to make my muffins and pot pies and live a quiet life here in Waverly." Jane was being dramatic, but she meant it.

"I'm glad to hear it. And your life doesn't have to be that quiet. There's always trivia."

Jane laughed. "That's about as wild and crazy and I want to get these days."

"Good, so does that mean we're on for tomorrow night?" Tuesday was trivia night at the pub.

"Sure, that sounds like fun."

"Great. I'll swing by for you at about six." Jake stood

up then to head off to work, but then he turned back and grinned. "Oh, and Jane. It *is* a date."

He left, and Jane was still smiling as she walked back to the register. Life in Waverly was very good indeed.

~The End~

ABOUT THE AUTHOR

Pamela M. Kelley lives in the historic seaside town of Plymouth, MA near Cape Cod and just south of Boston. She has always been a book worm and still reads often and widely, romance, mysteries, thrillers and cook books. She writes cozy mysteries and romances and you'll probably see food featured along with a recipe or two.